A Ready-Made
Amish Family

Jo Ann Brown

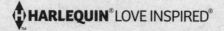

If you purchased this book without a cover you should be aware that this book is stolen property. It was reported as "unsold and destroyed" to the publisher, and neither the author nor the publisher has received any payment for this "stripped book."

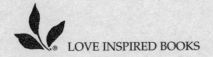

LOVE INSPIRED BOOKS

Recycling programs for this product may not exist in your area.

ISBN-13: 978-0-373-62272-6

A Ready-Made Amish Family

Copyright © 2017 by Jo Ann Ferguson

All rights reserved. Except for use in any review, the reproduction or utilization of this work in whole or in part in any form by any electronic, mechanical or other means, now known or hereinafter invented, including xerography, photocopying and recording, or in any information storage or retrieval system, is forbidden without the written permission of the editorial office, Love Inspired Books, 195 Broadway, New York, NY 10007 U.S.A.

This is a work of fiction. Names, characters, places and incidents are either the product of the author's imagination or are used fictitiously, and any resemblance to actual persons, living or dead, business establishments, events or locales is entirely coincidental.

This edition published by arrangement with Love Inspired Books.

® and TM are trademarks of Love Inspired Books, used under license. Trademarks indicated with ® are registered in the United States Patent and Trademark Office, the Canadian Intellectual Property Office and in other countries.

www.Harlequin.com

Printed in U.S.A.

Fear thou not; for I am with thee: be not dismayed; for I am thy God: I will strengthen thee; yea, I will help thee; yea, I will uphold thee with the right hand of My righteousness.

—*Isaiah* 41:10

For Stephanie Giancola

It's been more years than either of us want to admit since you sat down next to me at the first-timers' orientation (or did I sit down next to you?), and I've been blessed to enjoy your friendship ever since. All hail the Queen!

Chapter One

Paradise Springs
Lancaster County, Pennsylvania

"You look like you could use help."

When he heard the woman's calm voice, Isaiah Stoltzfus wanted to shout out his thanks to God for sending someone when he'd lost complete control of the situation. One *kind* was using the bellows in his blacksmith's shop to blow cold ashes everywhere, and two others clacked lengths of metal together like ancient knights holding sabers while a fourth *kind* sat on the stone floor and sobbed. In the past fifteen minutes, he'd learned the true meaning of being at his wits' end. He'd never guessed four young *kinder* could make him want to throw his hands into the air and announce he was in over his head. He'd been sure the *kinder* would be interested in visiting his blacksmith shop, but he'd been wrong. After a single glance around the space, they'd been bored and looked for the mischief they seemed able to find anywhere. He needed to take them somewhere else and find a way to divert their energy.

As if he'd given voice to his thoughts, Nettie Mae, the sobbing three-year-old girl sitting on his left boot, pressed her head against his leg and said, "Wanna go home, *Onkel* Isaiah. Go home now."

Before he could answer either Nettie Mae or the woman, a cloud of dust exploded out of his unlit forge. He sneezed and waved it away. The other three-year-old girl was pumping harder and harder until a wheezing warning sound came out of the leather bellows. He opened his mouth to tell Nettie Mae's twin, Nancy, to stop before she broke something, but one of the five-year-old boys who'd been poking at each other with the metal staffs yelped in pain and began crying.

Isaiah took a lumbering step toward the boys, hobbled by Nettie Mae, who clung like a burr to his trousers. How could he have lost control over four preschoolers so quickly?

The task wasn't one for a man who'd never had *kinder* of his own. Maybe if Rose hadn't died soon after they married and they'd had a *boppli*, it would be easier to anticipate what the youngsters might do next. The Beachy *kinder* were active and inquisitive, but every time he thought about scolding them, he recalled how they'd lost their parents two weeks ago. He didn't want to upset them more, yet somehow every situation escalated into pandemonium.

But the woman who had been a silhouette in the doorway didn't seem to have the same qualms. Without a single word, she walked into his smithy as if she'd been there dozens of times. A flash of sunlight danced on her lush, red hair, which was pulled back beneath her black bonnet. Her brown eyes glanced in his direction before she focused on the *kinder*. She plucked the shafts out of the boys' hands and scooped their sister off the cold forge in a single motion, scattering ashes across her own dark blue dress. Placing the metal bars on a nearby table, she settled Nancy on her hip and knelt in front of the boys.

"Where does it hurt?" she asked one twin—Andrew, Isaiah noted—as she wiped tears from his pudgy cheeks and almost dislodged his straw hat.

"Ouch," the towhead said, pointing to his right thumb that was already bright red.

Isaiah watched in amazement as the woman cradled the little boy's hand as she ran a fingertip along his thumb. When the *kind* flinched, she murmured something too low for Isaiah to hear, but Andrew must have understood because he nodded, his eyes wide and filled with more tears.

"I don't think it's broken," the woman said in the same serene voice, but loud enough so Isaiah could hear. "And I suspect as soon as little minds are focused on other things, the bruise will be forgotten. However, just in case, we should watch it over the next couple of days."

"We?" Isaiah asked, his voice rising on the single word.

"You *are* Isaiah Stoltzfus, aren't you?" She looked at the youngsters, then him. No doubt she was thinking there couldn't be another overwhelmed man with two sets of twins wrecking his smithy in Paradise Springs.

"*Ja*. Who are you?"

"Clara Ebersol."

"*You* are Clara Ebersol?" He shouldn't stare, but he couldn't help himself.

As she set Nancy on the floor and came to her feet, he held out his hand to help her. She must not have seen it, because she didn't take it. When she was standing, he was startled to realize he didn't have to look down far to meet her gaze. She was, he noticed for the first time, very tall for an Amish woman, because he wasn't a short man. None of the Stoltzfus brothers were, but her eyes were less than a handbreadth below his. She was also lovely—something he *had* already noticed—possessing a redhead's porcelain complexion. Not a single freckle marred her cheeks or dappled her nose.

He forced his eyes to shift away, glad nobody else was there. If he as much as talked to a woman for more than a minute, someone mentioned she would make him a *gut* wife. Everyone seemed eager to get their widowed minister married. Finding him staring at Clara Ebersol would have given the district's matchmakers cause to start sticking their well-meaning noses into his life again.

"Weren't you expecting me?" Clara stroked Andrew's hair, and the little boy leaned his head against her skirt. "Your brother Daniel learned I was looking for a job, and he asked me if I'd be willing to help you take care of these *kinder*. He said I'd find you here." For the first time, her composure showed a faint crack as she looked at him again. "Didn't he tell you?"

"*Ja*, he told me."

When Daniel had stopped at the Beachys' house on his way home a couple of nights ago, he'd been pleased to tell Isaiah that he'd found someone to help take care of the twins. Isaiah had been grateful when Daniel had said he'd talked to Clara Ebersol himself, and she seemed perfect for the job. Arrangements had been made for her to meet Isaiah at the smithy today, because he'd hoped to finish a few tasks. But what Daniel had failed to mention—and Isaiah had never thought to ask about—was that Clara Ebersol was not a well-experienced *gross-*

mammi who'd already raised a household of *kinder*. She was a lovely young woman. Was his brother, who'd recently fallen in love and found a family, matchmaking? That was the only reason Isaiah could think of why his brother hadn't mentioned Clara's age. If he had to guess, Isaiah would say she must be close to his thirty years.

Or had Daniel told him?

Isaiah wasn't sure he could recall anything during the past two weeks accurately. Maybe if he got a *gut* night's sleep, he'd be able to think. Every thought had to battle against the appalling memories of his friends' funeral playing over and over through his mind, refusing to be forgotten.

Reaching into the pocket of her black apron, Clara drew out four lollipops. The twins focused on her hand.

"I've got a red, an orange, a yellow and a green." She raised her head and asked, "Do they know their colors?"

Again Isaiah wasn't quick enough to answer, as Ammon, usually the quietest one, shouted, "Want that one!" He pointed to the red lollipop.

She squatted again and made sure each *kind* got the lollipop he or she wanted. Taking the cellophane off each piece of candy, she led the two sets of twins out of the smithy. She looked around, unsure where to have them eat their suckers.

The space between the long, low building that housed the Stoltzfus Family Shops and Isaiah's smithy was more cramped with each passing day. His brother Joshua's buggy shop was outgrowing its space. Last week, Joshua and his two older sons had spent hours setting up a canopy where buggies could be parked out of the weather until Joshua had time to fix them.

"How about over there?" he asked, pointing to the back step of the grocery store his brother Amos ran.

"Perfect." Motioning for the *kinder* to follow, she waited for each of them to select a spot on the concrete step. Once they were settled, the girls on one side and the boys on the other by unspoken consent, their tears and mischief were momentarily forgotten.

"Let's talk," he said, motioning for her to come back to him.

She hesitated, then walked to where he stood by the smithy's door. For a second, he wondered if she preferred the *kinder*'s company to his. Telling himself not to be foolish, because she didn't know any of them, he recognized he wasn't in any condition to make judgments. He was so tired he had trouble stringing more than three words together.

Quietly so her voice wouldn't reach the *kinder*, Clara said, "Your brother Daniel told me that they're orphans. That's terribly sad."

He nodded, words sticking in his tight throat. It had been only two weeks ago that he'd been roused out of bed in the middle of the night and learned his best friend Melvin Beachy had been killed along with Melvin's wife, Esta. They'd been traveling in an *Englisch* friend's truck coming home from an auction when something went wrong. The truck had gone through a guardrail and rolled, killing all three and leaving four small *kinder* without parents.

Nobody had been prepared for their deaths, but the whole community came together to help with the funeral. In the past two weeks, he hadn't made a single meal for the Beachy twins, because at least one person dropped by each day with casseroles and pies and fresh bread. As they had when his wife had died.

"I heard one of the girls call you '*onkel*,'" Clara went on when he didn't answer.

Relieved to be jerked out of his grim thoughts, he nodded again. "It's an honorary title. Their *daed* was my best friend, so the twins grew up with me around." He was surprised how *gut* it felt to talk about Melvin instead of avoiding any mention of either him or Esta as he had since their funeral. His family had been trying to tiptoe around the subject. Their efforts not to upset him were a constant reminder of what he'd lost. "Melvin asked me, after the girls were born, to be the *kinder*'s guardian in case something happened to him and Esta."

"They don't have any other family?"

"There are Melvin's parents and Esta's sister. But they are out of the country, working with Mennonite missions. The *kinder*'s grandparents, Melvin's parents, are in Ghana, and Esta's sister is in Chile. It'll take at least a month before they can return to Paradise Springs. Maybe longer for their *aenti* because a recent earthquake along the Chilean coast tore up many of the roads in the area where she's serving."

She smiled. "So you have become their temporary *daed*."

He wished he could smile, but grief weighed too heavily for his lips. "I moved into their house to take care of them until someone from their real family gets here. I figured it'd be easier for them than moving to my house."

He didn't add that disaster had followed disaster while he tried to keep up with the young and confused *kinder* who didn't understand why their parents had failed to come home as they'd promised. It hadn't taken more than a couple of days for Isaiah to realize he couldn't oversee them and run his blacksmithing business and fulfill his duties as a minister in the district. Neighbors and his family had been helping with the chores on the farm and in the house. Now that Clara was going to be at the house, she would tend to those jobs, and he could work in the barn without having the *kinder* out there with him. Keeping an eye on the little kids while trying to milk the family's dozen cows had been close to impossible.

"I should get to know them." She walked to the *kinder* and knelt in front of them.

Isaiah stayed where he was. The soft murmur of her voice drifted to him, but not her words. She seemed uncomfortable with him. If that was so, why had she taken the job? Again, he chided himself. He was in no condition to judge anyone or anything. If she could calm the *kinder* with such ease, then why would he care if she'd rather spend time with the twins?

But he did.

You're not thinking clearly. Be glad you've got help. And he was. Hoping he didn't fall asleep on his feet, he turned to the smithy and the task of cleaning the mess the youngsters had made.

Clara looked from the *kinder* who were enjoying their lollipops to Isaiah Stoltzfus as he walked with slow, heavy steps into the blacksmith's shop. The man was exhausted. He carried a massive burden of fatigue on his shoulders, and, if the half-circles under his eyes got any darker, he would look as if he were part raccoon. She guessed that when he wasn't so tired he was a *gut*-looking man. His brother had mentioned Isaiah was a widower. The beard he had started when he married remained thin in spots, or maybe its white-blond hair was so fine it was invisible at some places along his jaw. Above his snowy brows, the hair dropping over his forehead was several shades darker, a color she'd heard someone describe as tawny.

He seemed like a nice guy, but nice guys weren't always what they seemed. She'd learned that the hardest way. She didn't intend to make the mistake again.

Not getting too close or too involved was her plan. She would help him with the twins, and when their *aenti* or grandparents returned, she'd leave with a smile and her last paycheck. By then, maybe she would have figured out what she wanted to do in the future. It wasn't going to revolve around a man, especially a *gut*-looking one who could twist her heart around his little finger and break it.

A sharp crunch drew Clara's attention to the *kinder*. The two sets of twins looked enough alike to be quads. They had pale blond hair, the girls' crooked braids barely containing their baby fine tresses that floated like bits of fog. Another crunch came, and she realized one boy was chewing on his lollipop.

"Are those candies *gut*?" she asked, already seeing differences between the two boys. The boy with the injured finger had a cowlick that lifted a narrow section of his bangs off his forehead, and the other one had darker freckles.

"Ja," said one of the girls.

"I am Clara." She smiled as she took the empty sticks held out to her. "What are your names?"

The wrong question because the *kinder* all spoke at once. It took her a few moments to sort out that Andrew was the boy with the bruised finger and the other boy was Ammon. The toddler who had been climbing on the forge was Nancy, and her twin was named Nettie Mae.

She led them to a rain barrel at the end of the building and washed their hands and faces. Each one must have given the others a taste of his or her lollipop, because their cheeks had become a crazy quilt of red, orange, yellow and green. She cleaned them as best she could, getting off most of the stickiness.

As she did, first one *kind*, then the next began to yawn. She wondered if they were sleeping any better than Isaiah was. Or maybe they needed a nap.

Clara felt like a mother duck leading her ducklings as she walked to the blacksmith shop. A light breeze rocked the sign by the door that read Blacksmith. Peeking past the door, she saw Isaiah checking the bellows, running his fingers along the ribs. Did he fear Nancy's enthusiasm had damaged them?

Though she didn't say anything and the *kinder* remained silent, he looked up. He attempted a smile, and she realized what a strain it must be when he'd lost two dear friends.

"Is it all right?" she asked. When his forehead threaded with bafflement, she added, "The bellows?"

"They seem to be, but I won't know until I fire the forge."

"If it's okay with you, I'll take the twins home while you do what you need to here."

"I should show you where—"

"I think I can find my way around a plain kitchen," she said. She didn't want him to think she was eager to go, though she was. The fact she'd noticed how handsome he was had alarms ringing in her head. After all, her former fiancé, Lonnie Wickey, had been nice to look at, too.

"I'm sure you can," he said after she'd urged the *kinder* to get in her buggy. "But you should know the pilot light

on the stove and the oven isn't working. Do you know
how to light one?"

"*Ja.* Our old stove was like that." She lifted Nettie
Mae, the littlest one, into the buggy. "Did you have something planned for supper?"

"We've been eating whatever is in the fridge. I appreciate you coming to help, Clara." He glanced at where
the *kinder* were climbing into her buggy and claiming
seats. "Can you stay until their grandparents or their
aenti get here?"

"I can stay for as long as you need me to help with the
kinder." She didn't add she was glad to get away from
her *daed*, who found fault with everything she did. As
he had for as long as she could remember. Doing a *gut*
job for Isaiah could be the thing to prove to *Daed* she
wasn't as flighty and irresponsible as he thought. She
had been as a *kind*, but she'd grown up. Her *daed* didn't
seem to realize that.

"*Gut.*" His breath came out in a long sigh, and she realized he was more stressed than she'd thought. "If it's
okay with you, I'll finish some things here and get to the
farm in a couple of hours. You don't have to worry about
milking the cows. I'll do that after supper."

"Take your time. I know you haven't had much of it."

He gave her a genuine smile, and her heart did a peculiar little lilt in her chest. She dampened her reaction.

"*Danki,*" he said. "It's late, so getting set up for tomorrow is the best thing I can do. Firing the forge at this time
in the afternoon would take too long. With you here to
oversee the *kinder*, I'll be able to finish the commission
work that needs to be shipped by the end of next week."

Curious what he was making, she nodded and walked
to the buggy. She climbed in, pleased he didn't offer her

a hand in so that she didn't have to pretend—again—she hadn't seen his fingers almost in her face. She made sure the twins were settled, the girls on the front seat with her and the boys in the back where they could peer out the small rear window. Her two bags sitting on the floor between the seats wouldn't be a problem for their short legs.

Clara drew in a deep breath as she reached for Bella's reins. The bay shook her mane, ready to get to their destination after the hour-long drive from the Ebersol farm south of Paradise Springs. Clara was eager to be gone, too. Every turn of the buggy wheels took her toward her future, though she had no idea what that would be. The decisions would be hers, not some man's who made her a pledge, then broke it a few months later.

She had expected the little ones to fall asleep to the rhythmic song of the horse's iron shoes on the road, but getting into the buggy seemed to have revived them. When she glanced at the twins, she discovered four pairs of bright blue eyes fixed on her.

"You got *kinder*?" asked Nancy.

"No," she said, glad her black bonnet hid her face from them. Try as she might, she hadn't been able to keep her smile from wavering at the innocent question.

She had thought she would have a husband and be starting a family by now, but the man who had asked her to be his wife had married someone else in Montana without having the courtesy of telling her until after she'd found out from the mutual friend who had introduced them. Lonnie had come from Montana to visit Paradise Springs, and he'd courted her. Fool that she was, she'd believed his professions of love. Worse, he'd waited until he was married to write to her and break off their betrothal.

"I like you," said Nettie Mae, leaning her head against Clara's arm.

"I like you, too." Clara was touched by the *kind*'s words. They were what she needed.

"I got a *boppli*." She chewed on the end of her right braid.

"Will you show her to me when we get to your house?" Clara started to reach to pull the braid out of the *kind*'s mouth as she asked another question about Nettie Mae's doll, then stopped herself. There was time enough to help the youngster end a bad habit later. Chiding her wouldn't be a *gut* way to start with these fragile *kinder*.

The little girl nodded.

"Me, too," Nancy announced as she jumped to her feet.

Clara drew the horse to a walk, then looked at the excited little girl. "It's important we sit when we're riding in a buggy."

"Why?" both boys asked at the same time.

Worried that speaking about the dangers on the road might upset the twins and remind them of how their parents had died in a truck accident, she devised an answer she hoped would satisfy them. "Well, you see my horse? Bella is working very, very hard, and we don't want to make it more difficult for her by bouncing around too much in the carriage."

"Oh," said a quartet of awed voices.

"Like horse," Nancy said, sitting on the front seat again. "Pretty horse."

"*Ja*. Bella is a pretty horse." She slapped the reins and steered the carriage along the twisting road, making sure she watched for any vehicles coming over a rise at a reckless speed.

When a squirrel bounced across the road in front of

them, the kids were as fascinated as if they'd never seen one before. They chattered about where it might live and what it might eat and if they could have one for a pet.

"It's easy to catch a squirrel," Clara said. "Do you know how?"

"How?" asked Andrew, folding his arms on the top of the front seat.

"Climb a tree and pretend you're a nut." She waited for the *kinder* to laugh at the silly riddle, but they didn't.

Instead they became silent. The boys sat on the rear seat, and the girls clasped hands as Nettie Mae again began to chew on the end of her braid.

What had happened? They were old enough to understand the punch line, and she'd expected them to giggle or maybe groan. Not this unsettling silence.

"Where *Onkel* Isaiah?" Nettie Mae asked.

"Want *Onkel* Isaiah," whined her twin.

"We're going home to make supper for him," Clara said, keeping her tone upbeat.

"*Onkel* Isaiah make supper," Nettie Mae insisted.

"She's right," Andrew added. "*Onkel* Isaiah said he'd make supper until *Grossmammi* and *Grossdawdi* get home from 'freeca."

Glad Isaiah had explained the *kinder*'s grandparents were in Ghana, Clara was able to understand the boy's "'freeca" meant Africa. She struggled to hold on to her smile as she said, "But I offered to make supper tonight. It's nice to share chores sometimes, isn't it? Your *onkel* and I will be sharing the work."

"I'll help," crowed Andrew at the top of his lungs.

"Me, too!" shouted his twin.

Before Clara could ask them to lower their voices, Nettie Mae began to pout. "Me too little."

"Nonsense," Clara replied. "My *grossmammi* says God has work for all his *kinder*, no matter if they're young or old." She turned the buggy at a corner, following the directions Daniel Stoltzfus had given her. "Sometimes it means taking care of the beasts in the fields or making a nice home for our families. Other times, it's letting Him know we love Him. We can sing a song for God. Do you know 'Jesus Loves the Little Children'?"

"Ja!" they shouted.

She put her finger to her lips, but was relieved that they hadn't withdrawn as they had when she told the joke. "Do you know sometimes Jesus hears the song best if we sing quietly?"

"Really?" asked Andrew.

Already she could tell he was the one who spoke for his siblings. She suspected he was also their leader when they got into mischief.

"Ja," she answered. "Jesus listens to what's in our hearts, so when we sing quietly, it helps Him hear our hearts' voices."

Singing along with the youngsters, she watched for the lane leading to the Beachys' farm. Her hopes were high this job would be the perfect way for her to have time to decide what she wanted to do with the rest of her life. The *kinder* were easy to be around…as long as she kept them entertained. Their *onkel* would be busy with work, so she probably wouldn't see him other than at meals.

Driving up the lane toward the large white house with its well-kept barns set behind it, she imagined the first day her parents found money from her in their mailbox. She planned to send her pay home to her parents. Perhaps even *Daed* would be pleased with her efforts and acknowledge she wasn't a silly girl any longer. There was a first time for everything. Wasn't that what the old adage said?

Chapter Two

Clara kept the twins busy once they arrived at the Beachys' house and had put Bella in a stall in the stable out back. The boys' straw hats hung on pegs next to her bonnet by the door. The kitchen was a spacious room with cream walls and white cupboards. A large table was set near a bow window with a *wunderbaar* view of the dark pink blossoms ready to burst on the pair of crabapple trees. Every inch was covered with toys or stacks of dirty dishes.

When she asked the youngsters to pick up their toys and put them in the box in the front room, they kept her busy showing off their dolls and blocks and wooden animals and more trucks and tractors than she had guessed existed. She tried one more time to tell them a silly story, but again they became as silent as a moonless night.

What was she doing wrong? She must mention this to Isaiah when he returned to the house. Maybe after the *kinder* were in bed, though she'd be wiser to talk to him in the morning when the youngsters were focused on breakfast and paid no attention to the conversation.

Help me find the truth, Lord, she prayed as she put

another stack of dishes in the sudsy water and began washing them. The youngsters wanted to help, but she had visions of water splashed everywhere. Instead, she made up a game, and they arranged boots by size beside the door. The weather might be warm, but a good spring rain would turn the yard into mud. It'd be a few weeks before they'd put winter boots away in the cellar.

As the twins debated which boot went where as if it were a matter of the greatest importance, Clara hid her smile and finished the dishes. She took the youngsters upstairs so she could see their rooms after she had swept and mopped the kitchen floor. Once it dried, her shoes wouldn't stick to the wood on every step.

All the *kinder* slept in the same room. It was the breadth of the rear of the house, and she guessed from patches in the wood floor it once had been two rooms. Had their *daed* planned to put the wall up again once the twins were older? She silenced her sigh so she didn't upset her charges. Not that they would have noticed. One after another tugged on her hand, urging her to come and see the dresser and the pegs on the wall where their clothes hung or to look out the windows, both with a view of the fields beyond the barns and a pond. By summer, the frogs living there would sing a lullaby each night to soothe them to sleep.

The sound of the mantel clock downstairs tolling the hour interrupted Andrew, who was eager for Clara to see his coloring book.

"Time to make supper," she said.

"Me help!" Nancy and Nettie Mae cried at the same time.

"Everyone can help." She led the way down the stairs,

looking over her shoulder to make sure she was not going too fast for their short legs.

It wasn't easy, but Clara found jobs for each *kind* with setting the table or helping her find the bread, as well as telling her where the pickles were stored in the cellar. The twins were excited when she uncovered a bright red oilcloth in the laundry room and spread it over the table. Using it under the youngsters' plates would make cleaning up afterward simpler and quicker.

Once the twins were carrying spoons and plastic glasses to the table, she went to the refrigerator. As she'd expected, it was full of food brought by caring neighbors. She lifted out a large casserole pan. Peeling back one corner of the foil covering the dish, she discovered it was a mixture of tomato sauce, hamburger and noodles. She hoped the *kinder* and Isaiah would enjoy it. She was sure they would savor the chocolate cake she'd found in an upper cupboard. She lit the oven with matches from a nearby drawer, put the casserole in, set the timer and went to help the youngsters finish setting the table. Several glasses and two spoons hit the floor on the way to the table, but she rinsed them off and handed them back to the twin who'd been carrying them.

Soon a fragrant, spicy scent filled the kitchen. The casserole must contain salsa as well as tomato sauce. Her stomach growled, and the kids kept asking when supper would be served. She reminded them each time that they needed to wait for *Onkel* Isaiah. That satisfied them until they asked the same question thirty seconds later.

Hearing the unmistakable sounds of a horse-drawn buggy coming toward the house, Clara helped the *kinder* wash their hands. She scrubbed their faces clean before urging them to take their seats at the table. As the timer went off, she opened the oven and lifted out the casserole. She was putting it on top of the stove when the kitchen door opened and Isaiah walked in, the twins instantly surrounding him.

He started to speak, but a peculiar choked sound came out of him as he scanned the room as if he couldn't believe his eyes. He set his straw hat on an empty peg next to her bonnet and strode past the long maple table where the twins again sat. He paused between the gas stove and the kitchen sink, turned to look in each direction before his gaze settled on her.

"Am I in the right house?" he asked.

She couldn't help smiling in spite of her determination to keep Isaiah at arm's length. As long as the only thing between them was business, everything should be fine. "I hope so, because this is where your brother said to go, and we've spent the past two hours here."

He shook his head. "But there were dirty dishes everywhere when we left this afternoon, and my boots tried to cement themselves to the floor where the *kinder* had spilled food and milk."

"I know."

"How did you do all this in such a short time?" he asked as if he expected to see dirty dishes piled in a corner.

"Practice." She smiled at the *kinder*. "And plenty of eager hands to help."

He faced her, surprise in his eyes. "Those same hands make anything I try take two or three times longer than if I'd done the job by myself."

"I know a few tricks." She smiled. "I'm glad there are plastic glasses in the cupboard. Otherwise, I would have been sweeping up plenty of glass."

"*Ja*. They sometimes confuse glasses with a volleyball."

Her smile widened. "Wash up, and I'll get the food on the table. It'll be ready when you are."

When he glanced at her in astonishment, heat rushed up her face. She was acting as if she belonged there. It wasn't an impression she wanted to give him or anyone in Paradise Springs. As soon as he went into the bathroom, she busied herself getting milk from the refrigerator and filling each *kind*'s glass halfway. She needed to guard her words and remember she was the hired girl whose duties were to cook and clean and look after the *kinder*.

If Isaiah was bothered by what she'd said, he showed no sign when he walked into the kitchen. As he pulled out a chair, he said, "I'm amazed how fast you cleaned the kitchen. It took two of my sisters-in-law more than a day to set everything to order yesterday."

"The kitchen was cleaned yesterday?" She halted with the casserole halfway between the stove and the table.

"*Ja*. They came over to help."

Clara blurted, "You made such a mess in a single day?"

He arched a pale brow, and she laughed.

Sudden cries of dismay erupted from the twins, and Clara set the casserole on the stove. Had one of them gotten hurt? How? The shrieks threatened to freeze her blood right in her veins.

At the same time Isaiah jumped to his feet and hurried around the table to where the youngsters stood together in a clump as if trying to protect themselves from an unseen monster. Their eyes were huge in their colorless faces.

"What is it?" Isaiah asked, leaning toward them. "What's wrong?"

All four pointed at Clara. Shock riveted her. Were they insulted by her comment about the house becoming a disaster area in a day? No, they were barely more than toddlers. They didn't care about the state of their house.

"No laugh," said Nettie Mae around the end of her braid she'd stuck into her mouth again. She put her finger to her lips and regarded them with big, blue eyes. "Quiet and no laugh."

"No laugh. Quiet." Nancy pointed at Clara. "No laugh. Gotta be quiet."

Clara listened in appalled disbelief. Isaiah's face revealed he was as shocked as she was.

"Not laughing is hard," Andrew lamented. "Really, really hard."

"Squirrel funny, but no laugh," added his twin, his words coming out in an odd mumble. Was he trying not to cry? "Really, really hard no laughing."

"Really, really hard." Nettie Mae's lower lip wobbled, and a single tear slid down her plump cheek.

Clara gasped when Isaiah sat on the floor. He held out his arms, and the *kinder* piled onto his lap. But there was nothing joyous about them as they held onto him like leaves fighting not to be blown away by a storm wind.

"Tell me about the squirrel," Isaiah said. "I like funny stories."

Andrew shook his head, and his brother and sisters did, too. "No laughing. Be quiet."

"Who told you to be quiet?"

"She did." He pointed an accusatory finger at Clara. When Isaiah frowned, she said, "I asked them—"

"It's *gut*," Andrew said. "What Clara told us. To be quiet when we sing so Jesus can hear what's in our hearts."

Again Isaiah's pale brows rose, but his voice became

calmer as he replied, "That is true. Clara was very kind to help you learn that. Has anyone else told you to be quiet?"

"You!" Nancy poked one side of his suspenders.

He tapped her nose and smiled. "I've told you that a lot, because you make more noise than a whole field of crows, but you don't listen to me. You keep chattering away."

The twins exchanged glances, and Clara couldn't help wondering if they had some way to know what one another was thinking. She'd heard that twins seemed to be able to communicate without words, but had no idea if it was true.

"Tell me the story about the squirrel," Isaiah urged. "Did he chatter, too?"

Four small bodies stiffened. Nettie Mae chewed frantically on her braid, and Nancy's thumb popped into her mouth. The boys grabbed each other's hand and shook their heads.

"No laughing," Andrew whispered.

Clara squatted beside them and Isaiah. "Who told you that, Andrew?"

The little boy clamped his lips closed as his eyes grew glassy with tears. Beside him, his siblings' lips quivered.

When Isaiah started to speak, she put her hand on his shoulder to halt him. She wasn't sure if she was more astonished at her temerity or at the pulse of sensation rippling up her arm. She didn't want to be attracted to her employer—or any man—until she had sorted out what to do with her life. She wasn't going to make the same mistake of believing a man loved her and then being shown how wrong she was.

Pulling her hand back, she forced a smile. Now wasn't the time to worry about herself. She needed to focus on the *kinder*. "Let's have supper," she urged. "It'll taste better hot than cold." She made shooing motions, and the twins clambered onto their chairs.

She started to stand but wobbled. When Isaiah put a steadying hand on her back, she almost jumped out of her skin at the thud of awareness slamming into her so hard that, for a moment, she thought she'd fallen on the hard floor. She jumped to her feet as the *kinder* had and edged away so he could stand without being too close to her.

He asked quietly, "Do you have any idea what's going on with them?"

"You'd know better than I would. You've been around them their whole lives."

Gritting his teeth so hard she could hear them grind, he said, "My guess is, sometime during the funeral or the days leading up to it, someone they respect enough to listen to must have told them laughing was wrong."

"Who?"

"I don't know. You see how they don't always listen to me, and they love me. I've got no idea who might have told them not to laugh."

Why hadn't she seen the truth for herself? But who could imagine four little *kinder* would believe they shouldn't laugh again? When they'd become silent in the buggy, she'd known something was amiss.

But not this.

Putting her hand over her mouth before the sob bubbling up in her throat could escape, she turned away, not wanting them to see her reaction. "*Kinder* take everything at face value, so if someone told them not to laugh, they couldn't guess it meant only at the…" She gulped back the rest of what she was going to say. She didn't want to speak of their parents' funeral and cause further distress. "How much do they know about what's happened?"

He shrugged. "They attended the...the event."

"*Ja*, I assumed that." She was relieved he didn't say *funeral* or the names of the deceased. It was further proof he cared deeply about the twins.

"Who can guess how much a young *kind* understands?" His mouth grew straight. "I'm an adult, and I find it hard to believe my friends are gone."

"Are we going to eat?" called Andrew, again the spokesman for his siblings.

"Of course." Hoping her smile didn't look hideous, Clara slipped past Isaiah and went to get the casserole. "We don't want supper to get cold, do we?"

She placed the casserole dish in the middle of the table. She reached to pull out an empty chair next to where the girls sat on red and blue booster seats, but moved to another at the sight of the stricken expressions on the twins' faces. Nobody needed to explain the first chair was where their *mamm* used to sit.

Isaiah lifted Andrew out of his chair and moved him over one. Sitting between the two boys, he winked at them before bowing his head. Clara watched as the *kinder* folded their tiny hands on the table and lowered their eyes, as well. They had been well-taught by their parents. Looking from one to the next and at Isaiah, she closed her eyes and, after thanking God for their meal, prayed for Him to enter the Beachy twins' hearts and ease their grief.

And Isaiah's heart, too, she added when he cleared his throat to signal the time for silent grace was over.

The *kinder* dug into their meal with enthusiasm. Clara was sure it was delicious, because it'd smelled that way while heating. In her mouth, the meat and noodles tasted as dry and flavorless as the ashes on Isaiah's forge would have. She saw Isaiah toying with his food as well before scraping it onto the boys' plates when they asked for seconds.

He raised his eyes, and his gaze locked with hers across the table. In that instant, she knew what he was thinking. They needed to help the *kinder*. She agreed, but couldn't ignore how uneasy she was that she and Isaiah were of a mind. It suggested a connection she wasn't ready to make with a man again. She wasn't sure when she would be.

Maybe never.

Isaiah smiled, hoping the youngsters wouldn't guess he was forcing it. *Kinder* were experts at seeing through a ploy, so he tried to be honest with them. When Clara gave a slight nod, he hoped she shared his belief they had to help the twins laugh again.

He was astonished when she pushed back her chair and rose. She opened a cupboard and took down the chocolate cake Fannie Beiler had brought over yesterday. The Beilers lived next door to his *mamm*, and Fannie's daughter Leah was married to his brother Ezra. He'd stashed the cake away so the *kinder* didn't tease for it before they ate.

And then he forgot about it.

As Clara carried the cake to the table, the twins began squirming with anticipation of chocolate and peanut butter frosting. "Who wants a piece?"

"Me! Me! Me! Me!" echoed through the kitchen.

She smiled and took six small plates out of a lower cupboard. Setting them on the table, she cut the cake. She sliced four small servings and then put a plate in front of each *kind*. The piece she put in front of him was much bigger.

"Is that enough, Isaiah?" she asked. "Or do you want more?"

"How about if I say I want less?" he asked.

"I wouldn't believe you."

"And you'd be right." He fought not to chuckle, not wanting to distress the twins again.

"Don't wait for me," she said. "Try it."

The *kinder* needed no further urging. Within seconds, they were covered with chocolate crumbs and wearing broad smiles.

Though he was as eager as the twins to sample the cake, Isaiah waited for Clara to cut herself a small slice. He watched as she ate and glanced at the *kinder*, smiling at their silliness.

She was *gut* with them. He'd seen that from the moment she walked into his blacksmith shop and took control of the chaos. She had an intangible air of calm around her that seemed to draw the *kinder*'s attention so they listened to what she said.

And with her face not half-hidden beneath her bonnet, her hair rivaled the colors of the sunset. Somehow, her red strands weren't garish but more a reflection of the glow that transformed her face when she smiled. Really smiled, not a lukewarm one aimed at hiding her true feelings.

"Wasn't the cake *gut*?" Isaiah asked and was rewarded with four towheads bobbing together, though Ammon wasn't as enthusiastic at first. The youngsters must be exhausted. "Next time we see Fannie Beiler, you must tell her how much you enjoyed this cake."

"Yummy!" Nettie Mae said, patting her stomach. "Yummy in my tummy!"

A laugh, quickly squelched, came from where Clara sat beside the girls. She had her hand over her mouth and a horrified expression on her face.

He put hands on the boys' shoulders to keep them from running away from the table again. Clara had slipped her arm around the girls and started to apologize to them.

"No, don't say you're sorry," he hurried to say. "There's nothing wrong with laughing, right?" He looked at the boys.

Andrew nodded. "Clara can laugh, I guess."

"But not you?" she asked.

When the *kinder* remained silent, Isaiah pushed his plate away, though he hadn't finished the delicious cake. He folded his arms on the table.

"God wants us to be happy," he said as he looked from one young face to the next. "He loves it when we sing and when we pray together. Do you believe that?"

They nodded.

"And when we laugh together, too," he added.

The boys ran into the front room. When Nancy let out a cry, Clara drew her arm back from the girls who chased after their brothers and huddled with them by the sofa.

He wanted to go and comfort them, but wasn't sure what to say. He couldn't tell them they should accept the hurts in their lives because God had a plan for them to be happy in the future. He couldn't say that because he wasn't sure he believed it himself any longer. Since he'd learned of Melvin's and Esta's deaths, the uneasiness that had begun inside him after Rose's death had hardened his heart like iron taken from the forge. Every heartbeat hurt.

He struggled with his faith more each day. He believed in God, but it wasn't easy to accept a loving God would watch such grieving and do nothing. More than once, he'd considered seeking advice from his bishop, because he trusted Reuben Lapp as a man of God. But he knew what Reuben would say. Trust in God and be willing to accept the path God had given him to walk. Once he'd been happy to follow, but that was before Rose died from a severe asthma attack and then his friends' lives came to an end, leaving behind hurt and bewildered *kinder* who couldn't understand why the most important persons in their lives had gone away.

"Don't push them," Clara said from the other side of the table. "There's got to be a way to persuade them it's okay to laugh again like normal kids. I know there is."

"I wish I could be as sure."

When she stared at him, shocked a minister would speak so, he rose and went to the back door. He grasped his straw hat, put it on his head and said, "I've got to milk the cows. I'll be back in an hour or so."

He didn't give her time to answer. Striding across the yard to the big barn where the cows were waiting, he knew he needed to have an explanation for her when he returned.

He didn't know what it would be.

Chapter Three

When Isaiah came in after finishing the barn chores, the kitchen looked as neat as it had before supper. The room was empty, so he glanced toward the front room.

The twins were stretched out on the floor, coloring, while Clara sat on the sofa facing the wood stove and the rocking chair Melvin had bought for his wife when they first learned they were going to have a *boppli*. At that time, nobody had guessed Esta was carrying two *bopplin*.

He didn't move as Andrew got up and went to show Clara the picture he'd been working on. While she listened to the boy's excitement with the colors he'd chosen, she curved her hand across his narrow back, making a connection to the *kind*. Andrew was grinning when he dropped beside his sisters and brother. Clara returned to stitching a button on a shirt that must be from the pile of mending Esta kept in the front room.

It was the perfect domestic scene, one he'd believed he and Rose would one day share. The troubles they'd had in the first couple of months of their marriage had been behind them, and he'd been looking forward to building a family with her in the days before she died.

Alone.

Thinking of that single word was like swallowing a lit torch. There must have been a sign he'd missed, a wheezing sound when she breathed or a cough that went on and on or blueness around her lips. Something he should have seen and known not to go to work as if it were any other day. Something to tell him to stay home and comfort her and call 911.

He'd failed in his responsibility to her, and he couldn't make the same mistake with these youngsters. He owed that to his friends who had trusted him with their precious *kinder*.

Crossing the kitchen, Isaiah was surprised when the *kinder* were so focused on their coloring that they didn't raise their heads until Clara greeted him. She continued sewing, and he was astounded to see it was the shirt he'd lost a button on the other day.

"You don't have to do my mending." His voice sounded strained.

"I don't mind. I like staying busy." She looked at the *kinder*. "They've been coloring pictures for you."

"For me?"

She nodded, and he saw Andrew was coloring a bright red cow while his twin was using the same shade for a tractor. Nancy had been working on a blue bird with most of the strokes inside the lines, but Nettie Mae's page was covered with green with no regard for the picture of a dog in the middle of it. The little girl had her nose an inch from the coloring book.

When Nettie Mae paused to try to stifle a yawn, he had to wonder if she was half-asleep already. It had been a long day for the twins and an upsetting one, as well.

Clara stood and set his shirt on a table beside the sofa. "Time for baths."

The youngsters groaned, but gathered their crayons and put them in the metal box. She snapped the lid closed and picked up their coloring books while the twins asked what he thought of their pictures.

His answers must have satisfied them, though he couldn't recall a moment later what he'd said. His gaze remained on Clara as she set the books and crayon box on the lower shelf of a bookcase. The thin organdy of her *kapp* was warmed by her red hair. Every motion of her slender fingers seemed to be accompanied by unheard music.

When she turned, he didn't shift his eyes quickly enough. She caught him watching her, and the faint pink in her cheeks vanished. Was that dismay in her eyes? Dismay and another stronger emotion, but he couldn't discern what. As she had before, she lowered her eyes.

She remained on the other side of the room while she said, "Isaiah, I must get the *kinder* ready for bed."

"I'll give the boys their bath," he said, trying to lighten the situation. "I'll check behind all four ears."

His hope the twins would forget themselves and giggle was dashed, because they had become silent again. Did they sense the tension in the room? They couldn't know why. He didn't. He couldn't have said anything wrong, because he'd said less than a dozen words since he returned to the house.

But how was he going to convince the *kinder* it was okay to laugh? Though he and Clara had assured the twins a *gut* giggle would be all right, the twins continued to limit themselves to smiles.

I know I should be grateful they can smile, God, but a

kind *without a laugh seems wrong. You know what's in their hearts. Help me find a way into them, too, so their laughter can be freed.*

He understood why the youngsters might not trust Clara to release them from their promise not to laugh. They hardly knew her, though they seemed to like her.

And why wouldn't they like her? She was gentle and showed an interest in what mattered to them, acting as if each toy they showed her was the most amazing thing she'd ever seen. They wolfed down the food she put in front of them as if they hadn't eaten since birth.

But that didn't explain why the twins didn't heed *him*. He'd loved them before they were born. They called him *onkel*, and they were as close to his heart as his true nieces and nephews. Why didn't they trust him when he told them it was okay to laugh?

"I'll give the girls a bath," Clara said, "and checking behind ears sounds like a *gut* idea." She took a single step toward him, then paused. "Are there two bathrooms in the house?"

"We'll use the bathroom in the *dawdi haus*." He took the boys' hands. "Don't worry. My sisters-in-law cleaned it yesterday, and I moved my stuff over there."

"You're staying in the *dawdi haus*?"

"Is that a problem?"

For a moment, he thought she was going to say *ja*, but she replied, "I assumed you would stay at your house."

He let go of the boys' hands and crossed the room so he could lower his voice to keep the *kinder* from overhearing. "Clara, you've got to understand. Melvin and Esta expected me to take care of their family, and I won't let them down. When Daniel told me you'd agreed to come and help, I decided I'd use the *dawdi haus*. With the door between us and four very nosy chaperones—" He made a silly face at the twins who'd tiptoed over to listen.

Again they didn't giggle, though they smiled. It seemed bizarre to have young *kinder* acting restrained.

"You think," Clara finished for him, "that will keep tongues from wagging."

"These are extraordinary circumstances as well as temporary ones. Everyone knows that. However, if you're uncomfortable, I won't ask you to stay."

"Stay, Clara!" shouted Andrew, bouncing from one foot to the other. "You said we can make cookies tomorrow."

"I can ask *Mamm* to come while we look for someone else," Isaiah continued as if the little boy hadn't spoken. "She planned to help, but she had a bout with pneumonia last month. She's not completely recovered. That's why my brothers and I thought it was better to hire someone."

"You need my help, and I'm here." She held out her hands to the girls. "Let's get you fresh and clean."

As she started to walk past him, Isaiah said, "*Danki*, Clara." He pointed toward a door between the refrigerator and the stove. "Just so you know, the *dawdi haus* is through there. You're welcome to use the downstairs bedroom by the bathroom."

"I'm sorry to take it from you."

"I didn't use it."

Her earth-brown eyes grew round. "Because it was where…" She glanced at the girls who were listening to every word. "It was where your friends slept?" She gave him a sad smile. "Aren't there more bedrooms upstairs?"

"*Ja*, two, but they're used for storage."

"Is there a bed in one?"

"*Ja*, in both."

"Then I'll use the one close to the *kinder*'s bedroom door. I think it'd be better for me to be on the same floor with them."

He glanced at the boys, who had gotten bored and were pulling blocks out of the toy box. "That's a *gut* idea. I slept on the sofa, and I was up there most nights several times."

"Nightmares?"

"Either that, or they couldn't sleep." He grimaced. "I hate that you'll be taking care of them while I'm sleeping in the *dawdi haus*."

"It's what you're paying me for." She spoke the words without any emotion and walked with the girls toward the bathroom.

He wasn't sure what he would have said if she hadn't left him standing in the middle of the front room.

After he'd finished cleaning the puddles in the *dawdi haus* bathroom left by two little boys, Isaiah returned to the main house. He went upstairs and waited by the twins' bedroom door. He said nothing as Clara finished reading a story. The *kinder* listened, rapt, to the tale of a naughty bunny who learned a lesson through misadventures. He held his breath each time a little one raised a hand to an eye. Each time, the *kind* was trying to rub away any sleep catching up with him or her before the charming story was over.

He forced his shoulders to relax. He needed to stop overreacting to everything the twins did, assuming their tears had to do with grief instead of a bumped knee and being sleepy. He needed to be more like Clara, who kept them entertained but allowed for quiet moments, as well. He could see he'd been winding them up tight in an effort to prevent them from thinking about their parents. He shouldn't have been surprised they'd acted badly at his blacksmith's shop.

Being too busy to think hadn't worked for him either. No matter how many tasks he tried to concentrate on, he couldn't forget the gigantic hole in his life. How many times in the past couple of weeks had he thought of something he wanted to tell Melvin? Each time, renewed anguish threatened to suffocate him.

"Do you want to *komm* in and say a prayer with us?" Clara called as she knelt with the *kinder* by one of the small beds.

Joining them, Isaiah listened to their young voices saying the prayer they spoke every night. Clara asked if they wanted to ask for God's blessing on anyone special.

Andrew, always the leader, said, "*Onkel* Isaiah."

"Clara," added Nettie Mae, smiling at her.

But the smiles vanished when her twin said, "*Mamm* and *Daed* in heaven with You."

The pressure of tears filled his eyes, but he blinked them away as he lifted Ammon and set him on his bed before doing the same with Andrew. He tucked them in after they kissed him *gut nacht*. He turned to check on the girls. They were already beneath their covers, but he leaned over to collect kisses from them. All four insisted on giving Clara a kiss, too.

"Sleep well and have pretty dreams," she said as she turned down the propane lamp so a faint glow came from it.

He walked out with her, and she left the door open a finger's breadth. "That was a cute story," he said. "The twins were enthralled, though they've probably heard it a dozen times."

"No, they haven't. I brought the book with me." She glanced at the door, then followed him down the stairs. "I brought several along. Reading them a story that their *mamm* or *daed* read could be too painful for them."

He relaxed his shoulders, letting some of his worry slide away. Maybe this would work out. Clara was tender with the *kinder*, thinking of their needs and trying to keep them from more pain.

He urged her to contact him if she needed anything, then said, "*Gut nacht*, Clara."

"*Gut nacht*," she replied before she went into the bathroom. She didn't close the door, and he guessed she was gathering the wet towels left from the girls' bath.

Going into the *dawdi haus*, he shut the door to the kitchen behind him. He faltered, then threw the sliding lock closed. Anyone seeing it would realize he and Clara intended on maintaining propriety.

Isaiah lit a lamp in the small living room that had two other doors opening off it. One was to the bathroom, the other to the cozy bedroom. Picking up his extra boots, he set them by the door he'd be using except when he went to the main house for meals or to spend time with the twins.

A light flickered outside the living-room window, startling him until he recognized the easy stride of Marlin Wagler, the district's deacon. If Marlin went to the main house, he could disturb the *kinder* whom Isaiah hoped were asleep. He grabbed a flashlight and hurried outside. He waved the light, catching the deacon's eye.

He wondered why the deacon was calling tonight. The deacon's duties revolved around making sure the *Leit* followed the district's *Ordnung* as well as handling money issues, helping any member of the community pay medical bills or appointing people to arrange fund-raisers to provide for those who needed extra assistance. He hoped the problem was a simple one, because he didn't know how long he'd be able to focus on anything complicated tonight.

"*Komm* in," he said with a smile.

"I didn't expect to see you in the *dawdi haus*," Marlin said as he switched off his flashlight and walked in.

The deacon was a squat man, almost as wide as he was tall. Since he'd handed over the day-to-day running of his farm to his youngest son, Marlin had gained more weight. He was about the same age as Isaiah's late *daed* would have been. What hair remained on his head clung in a horseshoe shape from one ear to the other. It had turned gray years ago.

"Let's sit," Isaiah answered, "and you can tell me why you're here."

Marlin sat with a satisfied sigh in the overstuffed chair closer to the door. Once Isaiah had taken the other seat, Marlin began speaking of news from throughout the district and beyond. After he finished farming, he'd taken a job giving tourists buggy rides to his family's farm. He had amusing tales to share about the outrageous questions visitors asked.

"I've got to explain over and over," the deacon said with a chuckle that shook his broad belly, "we're not part of a living museum. We're just living our lives. However, I've recently driven people who seem to understand that. It's a blessing to be able to answer sensible questions."

"But those tourists don't make for *gut* stories."

"No, but they make for a pleasant day."

"I'm sure." Isaiah intended to add more, but a knock on the connecting door brought him to his feet. Sliding the lock aside, he opened it. Belatedly he realized he should have explained the situation to Marlin already.

Dear Lord, give me a gut night's sleep tonight. I'm no longer thinking straight.

"Excuse me." Clara clasped her hands in front of her. "I didn't mean to interrupt. I was wondering what time you wanted breakfast, Isaiah."

"*Komm* in." He motioned toward his other guest. "This is Marlin Wagler, our district's deacon. Marlin, this is Clara Ebersol."

"Oh," Marlin said, "I thought you might be the *kinder*'s *aenti* Debra. I've been looking forward to meeting her."

"It'll be several weeks, maybe as much as a month, before Debra will be able to get here from Chile." He'd never met Debra Wittmer whose home was in California when she wasn't away on mission work.

"Meanwhile," Clara said with a smile, "I'm here as a nanny for the *kinder.*"

Marlin smiled. "*Gut.* They need a stable home. What a blessing your family and your young man don't mind you being away."

"I don't have a young man," Clara said, blushing so brightly her face was almost the color of her hair.

"No?" Marlin glanced at Isaiah and arched a brow.

"Will five be too early for breakfast?" Isaiah asked before the deacon could add anything else. He hadn't expected Marlin to start quizzing Clara about her personal life. It was, Isaiah was sure, an attempt at matchmaking.

"Five will be fine. I'll have breakfast ready then. *Gut nacht.*" She shut the door, not hiding her yearning to escape before she embarrassed herself again.

He heard her fading footsteps. Taking a deep breath, because Marlin was sure to have questions, Isaiah said,

"Before you say anything, I'm living in the *dawdi haus*, as you can see." He hooked a thumb toward the stacks of clothing he'd brought from the main house. "With four very young *kinder*, I'm staying nearby in case Clara needs help with something. Though she's already shown she can take care of the household better than I could."

"I assume Reuben approves of this plan."

"Ja," he replied. As soon as his brother had told him about Clara, Isaiah had gone to the bishop and shared the plan with him. Of course, at that time, he hadn't known Clara Ebersol was a beautiful young woman.

It doesn't matter, he told himself. He wasn't looking for someone to court, and Clara was at the house for one reason: to take care of the *kinder*.

"Gut," Marlin said, his smile widening.

Isaiah wanted to groan aloud. He recognized the twinkle in the deacon's eye. Marlin and Atlee Bender, the other minister in their district, had been getting less and less subtle in their pressuring for Isaiah to choose another wife. They believed an ordained man should be married. It was a requirement for one's name to be put into the lot when a new minister was chosen, but nobody could have guessed Rose would die so soon after Isaiah was selected. Both men had told him that he'd had enough time to mourn, and finding a wife should be a high priority for him. They seemed to think it was as easy as going to his brother's grocery store and selecting one off the shelf.

Even if it was that simple, he wasn't interested in risking his heart and the devastating pain of loss again.

Clara slipped into the front bedroom across from the twins' bedroom door. It was crowded with boxes and cast-off furniture as Isaiah had warned. Trying to be quiet, she moved quilts and unused material from the bed. The mattress was clean, and she found sheets and a pillow in a cupboard in the hallway.

She made the bed, covering it with the topmost quilt from the pile. After braiding her hair, she went to the bed. Pulling back the bright red, blue and purple nine-patch quilt and the sheet beneath it, she sat on the edge of the bed and plumped the pillow.

Lying down, she watched the moonlight filtered by the leaves of the tree outside the window. It danced, making new patterns with every shift in the breeze.

The day had not gone badly, other than the shocking revelation by the *kinder* that they'd been told not to laugh. The twins seemed to accept her as part of their lives…so far. And she hadn't insulted Isaiah—or she thought she hadn't—so far. She must keep everything impersonal between them, as she would with anyone who hired her. Though he'd been puzzled when she spoke to him from the other side of the front room, he hadn't said anything.

Thank You, Lord, for keeping Isaiah from asking questions. She started to add to her prayer, but paused when she heard something. The noise was so soft she wasn't sure if she'd heard it. Then it came again.

A sob.

One of the *kinder* was crying.

Kicking aside her covers, Clara leaped out of bed. She grabbed the flashlight she'd left on the windowsill. She bumped into a stack of boxes, but kept them from tumbling to the floor. The big toe on her right foot hit the frame around the door, and she bit her lower lip to keep from making a sound. Limping across the hall, she aimed the flashlight against her palm and switched it on.

Its glow gave her enough light to see without being so bright it woke any *kinder* who were asleep.

Her aching toe was forgotten when she heard another sob. It led her to where Ammon was lying on his left side with his knees drawn up to his chest as if in grave pain. She leaned over and spoke gently. He didn't respond, just kept sobbing.

Wanting to soothe him, she lifted Ammon off the bed and carried him out of the room before he woke his brother and sisters. She kept the flashlight pointed at the floor as she eased down the unfamiliar stairs and into the living room. Lighting the propane lamp while she held him took twice as long as it normally would, but she didn't want to release the *kind*. Not when he was sobbing as if he believed nothing in his life would ever get better.

She went to the rocking chair in front of the unlit wood stove. Sitting, she began to rock as she settled Ammon's left cheek over her heart. She spoke to him, but when her words seemed to offer him no comfort, she began humming the song she'd sung with the *kinder* in the buggy. She meant it as a prayer, wanting Jesus to fill Ammon's heart with His love and reassurance. Slowly the little boy's body relaxed, molding to her. She kept rocking as he closed his eyes, a longer time coming between each sob.

Hearing a soft click from the kitchen, Clara looked over her shoulder. Isaiah walked toward her, his face lengthening when he saw the *kind* in her arms.

"I saw the light," he whispered. "Is everything all right?"

"It will be." She glanced at the *kind* cuddling close to her. Ammon had fallen asleep. "I thought he'd had a bad dream. I heard him crying and went to check. He wasn't asleep. I think he's missing…." As she had before, she chose her words with care, knowing if she said "*mamm*" and "*daed*," she might rouse the little boy. "He wants those who aren't here."

"What about the others?"

"Asleep when we came down."

"That's a blessing." He turned a chair around and sat, facing her. "They went to bed tonight for you better than they have for me."

"They're exhausted." She didn't pause as she added, "You are, too. You should get some sleep while you can."

"A few more minutes won't matter, and that guy is pretty heavy for you to tote upstairs. I don't want you stumbling and getting hurt."

"I appreciate that."

Standing, he held out his arms. "Let me take him."

As Isaiah leaned toward her, Clara realized her mistake. When he lifted Ammon out of her arms, Isaiah's face was a finger's breadth from hers. She held her breath and kept her eyes lowered while they made the transfer. Isaiah's work-roughened fingers brushed against her skin, sending heat along it.

As soon as he took Ammon upstairs, she pushed out of the rocker. She gripped the top of it, her knuckles turning white, as she fought for equilibrium. She couldn't react like this every time a casual touch brought her into contact with Isaiah. She gripped the chair and was trying to slow her heart's frenzied rhythm when he came back down the stairs.

Her hope that Isaiah wouldn't notice her bleached fingers was dashed when he said, "I'm sorry, Clara, for Marlin asking you if you're walking out with someone. He can't seem to help himself sticking his nose into matters he believes are his responsibility."

"That's a deacon's job," she said, not wanting to speak of how she scurried away like a frightened rabbit in a hedgerow.

"*This* deacon's job seems to be focused on finding me another wife." With the cockeyed grin Isaiah seemed to wear whenever he was trying to be self-deprecating, he sighed. "I'm sorry. I know you didn't figure on being the subject of matchmaking when you took this job."

"I don't like matchmaking."

"I agree. One hundred percent."

She appreciated his blunt answer and that he hadn't asked her to explain her comment. She didn't want to tell him that she was too well acquainted with matchmaking and the heartbreak it could cause.

"Clara, don't worry. We'll ignore everyone's match-making." He walked toward the door to the *dawdi haus* before facing her again. "In a way, we should be grateful to Marlin for bringing the subject out in the open, so neither of us has to act like we need to hide something."

"Ja," she said, as he urged her to try to have a *gut* night's sleep.

He closed the door, and she heard the lock slide into place. She reached for her flashlight. Her fingers trembled as she picked it up and turned off the lamp. She hadn't been honest with Isaiah. She already was hiding something from him. The way her heart took a lilting leap whenever he touched her.

"You can jump about all you want," she whispered to her traitorous heart while she climbed the stairs. "There's nothing you or anyone else can do to change my mind. I won't be made a fool of by another man. Not ever again."

Chapter Four

$\sim$

As the sun rose the next morning, Isaiah finished his second cup of *kaffi* and put the empty cup beside his plate with a regretful sigh. Clara brewed *kaffi* strong, as he liked it when he had a long day ahead of him. He'd already finished milking the cows and let them out in the meadow as well as feeding the chickens and the horses. He wanted to finish the final upright for a double gate ordered by an *Englisch* horse breeder in Maryland. He needed to make a few curled pieces and a half dozen twisted lengths to complete the pattern. When the gates were finished, they would be shipped to the man's farm to be hung on either side of a driveway. A truck was collecting it at the end of next week.

With Clara's arrival, he should be able to finish the job on time. He couldn't let her delicious French toast tempt him to have another serving and linger at the table with her and the Beachy twins. The *kinder* were eating their second servings, dripping maple syrup and melted butter on the oilcloth Clara had spread across the table before serving breakfast. Seeing Nettie Mae dipping her fingers in the syrup and then licking them, he smiled. She caught him looking at her and grinned.

"Yummy, isn't it?" he asked.

"Yummy, yummy, yummy in my tummy, tummy, tummy."

"Is that your new saying, Nettie Mae?"

"*Ja.* Yummy in my tummy." She turned the phrase into a little song.

"I see happy faces. What did I miss?" Clara asked as she brought a new stack of steaming, eggy toast from the stove. She set the platter next to him.

"Nettie Mae said the toast is yummy in her tummy," Isaiah replied. "And she's singing about it."

"And a fun tune it is, too. More *kaffi*?"

He pushed back his chair and stood. "*Danki*, but I need to get to work."

"Do you come home for dinner at midday?" Clara asked, sitting where she had the night before.

"I've been since…" He glanced at the *kinder* who were too intent on their French toast to pay attention to the conversation.

"I can move the main meal to the evening if it's easier for you."

"I appreciate that. Once the forge is at the right temperature, I don't want to cool it down and have to wait to reheat it again. I appreciate your flexibility, Clara."

She shrugged off his compliment. "Anything else I should know about your work schedule?"

"Usually I am done around four. That allows me time to milk the cows and get cleaned up before the evening meal."

"I'll have dinner ready around six."

"*Gut.*" He stamped down the thought that Clara had

avoided joining them at the table until he got up to leave. That wasn't fair to her. She'd been busy preparing breakfast and trying to stay ahead of four enthusiastic youngsters who seemed to have bottomless stomachs. But he couldn't ignore how, when he looked at her, it was as if he faced a closed door.

"Will you need a lunch packed for today?"

He motioned for her to stay where she was. "I'll get something at Amos's store today. You finish your breakfast before it's cold."

Going to the door, he took his straw hat off the peg above the low row where smaller hats and bonnets waited for the *kinder*. He put it on his head and reached for the doorknob.

"*Onkel* Isaiah!" cried Nancy as she jumped up.

Her booster seat slid forward, pushing her toward the table. Her elbow hit her plate, and everything seemed to move in slow motion. The plate flipped into the air, spraying maple syrup everywhere. Her unfinished slice of toast struck her glass and knocked it into her sister's. Both glasses bounced and rolled onto Andrew's plate before coming to a stop in the middle of Ammon's. More syrup and melted butter flew across the table.

Clara grabbed the boys' glasses and kept them from falling over and spilling more milk on the table. The *kinder* tried to help, but ended up with more food on them and across the chairs. A plate fell off the table and clattered on the floor. It landed upside down, one corner of toast peeking out from beneath it.

Silence settled on the kitchen as they stared at the mess. He heard a muffled sound and glanced at Clara. She was biting her lower lip to keep from laughing.

"Now I understand how the kitchen could get messy

in a single day," she said. "Maybe I should have put the oilcloth on the floor instead of on the table."

Isaiah had to put his hand over his mouth to stifle his laugh. The *kinder* were smiling, but exchanging the uneasy looks he realized were their way of reminding each other not to laugh. He lost any desire to give into the humor of the situation. There was nothing funny when four little kids refused to let themselves act as *kinder* should.

Who'd told them not to laugh? Once he found out, he was going to have that person explain to the twins he or she had made a big mistake. It was *gut* for them to laugh. They needed to express their happy emotions as well as their sad ones.

But they aren't showing those either. That thought unsettled him more. How could he have failed to notice? Caught up in the day-to-day struggle to balance taking care of them with his work at the forge, he'd been too focused on each passing minute to look at the bigger picture.

Hanging his hat on the peg, he ran to the sink and grabbed the dishrag. He wet it, wrung it out and began pushing the puddles of syrup from the edge of the table. The cloth became a sticky mess within seconds. Tossing it into the sink, he grabbed the roll of paper towels.

"*Komm*, and let's get cleaned up." Clara motioned for the *kinder* to follow her toward the bathroom.

Placing paper towels over the puddle of milk and syrup, Isaiah started to dab it up.

"Leave it," Clara said. "We'll clean it once there are a few less layers of syrup on us."

"Let me get started so no more hits the floor."

"Danki." Her smile warmed him more than another

cup of her delicious *kaffi*. Before he could smile back, she'd turned to the wide-eyed twins. "Pick up your plates and put them in the sink on your way to the bathroom. Don't touch anything else!"

The abashed *kinder* obeyed without a peep, astonishing Isaiah anew. They'd done as he asked, though not always as he'd hoped. And the results had often been another disaster on top of the one he was trying to get put to rights.

Isaiah went to work cleaning the table and the floor while he listened to Clara helping the twins wash in the bathroom. Later, when the youngsters were in bed and couldn't hear, he needed to ask her how she persuaded them to obey her.

He finished catching the last drip of butter off the oilcloth as the door opened. Assuming it was one of his brothers, stopping on the way to work, he gasped out loud when he saw a petite woman stepping into the kitchen.

"*Gute mariye*, Isaiah. I'm here to help you and..." She glanced around the kitchen, and her eyes widened. "It's clean! Except for the mess at the table, I mean."

"*Ja*, it's mostly clean." It took every bit of his strength to keep his smile in place. It wasn't Orpha Mast's fault her voice was too much like her sister Rose's. Putting his finger to his lips, he grimaced as he tasted syrup. "And please not so loud. The *kinder* went to wash their hands, and if they realize someone's visiting, they'll come running and drip water all the way."

"The little ones are washing their hands by themselves?" Orpha waved aside his answer. "Never mind. It won't take long to wipe up the bathroom. It's only soap and water, ain't so?"

"They aren't—"

Not allowing him to explain, she gave him a sympathetic smile. "You look better than the last time I saw you."

"I'd just finished speaking over the graves of my best friend and his wife."

She tilted her head so she could eye him with a sad smile. "You have such a burden to carry, Isaiah. Your work, your obligations to the district and four little ones. You don't have to do it on your own, you know."

"I know. I—"

"You know you can ask for help," she said, not letting him finish again.

"I know. I—"

"Those who want to help are right in front of you." The hint of a smile curved along her perfect lips. "Let me help you, Isaiah. I would do anything for you. Ask me, and I'll be by your side to take care of these *kinder*."

He was saved from having to answer the unanswerable when the twins poured out of the bathroom, holding up their hands to show him they were clean. He had his back to the bathroom door, but he knew the moment Clara stepped into the room because Orpha's smile became brittle.

"Who is *she*?" his sister-in-law asked so crisply the twins halted and stared.

Pretending not to hear the venom in Orpha's voice, Isaiah said, "Orpha, this is Clara Ebersol. She's here to take care of the *kinder*. Clara, this is my sister-in-law, Orpha Mast."

"How kind of you to come and check on Isaiah and the *kinder*," Clara said with a smile.

Had she missed Orpha's tone? Unlikely. Clara already seemed able to discern what he was thinking far too often. She was being nice, he realized, and trying to defuse the situation. Why didn't Orpha see that her sharp words were upsetting the twins?

"I guess I don't need to check on them if you're here," Orpha replied in the same clipped tone. "Are you related to the Beachys?"

"No." Clara folded a damp towel over her arm. "We're about to sit back down for the rest of our breakfast. Would you like to join us?"

Say no, Isaiah begged in his thoughts.

"No." Orpha glared at all of them. "It would appear I'm not needed here." Without another word, she left, closing the door harder than necessary.

"Why was her face like a duck's bill?" asked Andrew as he stuck out his lips in an imitation of Orpha's exasperated expression. "Did she taste something bad?"

"We'll never know, will we?" Clara steered the youngsters to the table. "Who would like more French toast?"

The twins climbed into their chairs and booster seats. They began chattering as if there hadn't been any interruption, and Clara went to the stove. Isaiah put the paper towels he was holding in the trash.

"I'm sorry," he said. "Orpha was surprised to see you here."

"She was." Clara didn't look at him. "Don't worry about it. I know you've got a lot to do at the blacksmith shop."

"I do, but..." He raked his fingers through his hair, then grimaced when he realized syrup still stuck to them. Too late to worry now. "The folks around here are pretty friendly."

"I'm sure they are," she said in the same calm tone as she set two slices of bread on the griddle. She stepped back as egg sizzled and snapped. "Your sister-in-law isn't happy with me being here."

"You don't have to put it politely. Orpha wants me to walk out with her. I don't know how many times she's mentioned being a minister's wife must be interesting." He grimaced. "Her description, not mine."

"Perhaps you should go after her and tell her she doesn't have to worry about me being her competition." She arched a single brow.

Fascinated, because he'd never been able to make that motion, he replied, "That would begin a conversation I'd prefer to avoid."

"And more matchmaking?"

"I hope not." He gave her a wry smile. "There's already enough of that going on because her *mamm* likes to arrange marriages for her daughters."

She started to smile back, then looked toward where the *kinder* were eating with enthusiasm. Turning to the stove, she didn't say anything.

He didn't either. The problem of unwanted matchmakers was nothing compared to what the twins faced growing up without their loving parents. He needed to remember that. Matchmaking was an annoying irritant that he could—that he *must*—ignore. Everything he did and everything he thought about should be focused on four small *kinder* who now depended on him and Clara.

The *kinder* were upset when Isaiah didn't come home for lunch as he had every day since the funeral, but Clara distracted them by letting them help her make church spread sandwiches for their midday meal. Soon peanut butter and marshmallow whip stuck to their hands, their faces and the table. She kept it from their clothes by tying aprons around their necks.

Serving potato chips and milk to them and getting fresh ice tea for herself, she joined the *kinder* at the table. They yawned while they gobbled their food as if they hadn't had breakfast a few hours before. A morning spent picking up the mess in their shared bedroom had tired the youngsters…as she hoped. A *gut* nap this afternoon would allow her time to check the cellar and see what food was stored there. The dishes left in the freezer could be part of a meal, not the whole thing.

The twins' naptime seemed to fly by, and she'd finished inventorying about half of the canned fruit, vegetables and meat in the cool cellar. Tomorrow, she would count the rest, but she was relieved to see there was plenty of food for the next four to five weeks until their family came to get the twins. She'd also found bottles of root beer with no date on them. Maybe Isaiah would know when Esta had bottled it. If it was *gut* to drink, the *kinder* would enjoy the treat.

Clara was coming down the stairs with the twins when she heard the door open. Sending up a prayer Orpha Mast hadn't decided to return, Clara hurried through the living room to see who was calling.

A short woman with gray lacing through her brown hair stood next to a gray-haired man with the bushiest eyebrows Clara had ever seen.

"Are you Clara?" asked the woman.

"I am."

"I'm Wanda Stoltzfus. Isaiah's *mamm*. I wanted to stop by and see how you're doing." Her round face split with her smile. "And I brought chocolate chip cookies."

The *kinder* cheered and danced around her. When Clara reached to grab little hands, the man grinned.

"They're fine," he said in a deep voice that resembled distant thunder. "Trying to catch them is like trying to capture a clutch of chicks. Oh, I guess I should introduce myself. I'm Reuben Lapp."

She recognized the name of the local bishop. "I'm glad to meet you. Let me put on the kettle. Or would you rather have *kaffi*?"

"Tea would be *gut*," the bishop said. "Ice tea if you have it."

"I made some this morning when it appeared the day was going to be hot."

"Summer is early this year." Wanda gestured with her plate of cookies. "Shall we enjoy these outside? Then the birds can have the crumbs instead of giving Clara another reason to sweep the floor." She smiled over the youngsters' heads. "I assume you've already swept at least twice today."

"Three times, but who's counting?" She regretted the words as soon as she spoke them, because Reuben let out a guffaw.

The *kinder* stared at him, not sure if the sound had been a laugh or a cough or a sneeze. Before they had time to react further, Clara shooed them and her guests out the front door. She would explain to the bishop and Wanda about the twins and their fear of laughter, but she didn't want to when the youngsters could overhear.

Diverted by the cookies, the twins followed Wanda and Reuben onto the porch. The sound of their voices drifted to Clara as she filled glasses with ice tea for the adults and cool water for the *kinder*. There were enough plastic ones for everyone, which was a relief. She didn't want one of the barefoot twins bumping a glass and leaving shards on the porch.

She brought the glasses out on a tray. Wanda and the bishop were seated on the porch. The twins were kicking a ball around the front yard under their watchful eyes.

Serving the ice tea to her guests and setting the tray on a small table beside the cookies, Clara sat on the glider at the far end of the porch. She took a grateful sip as she realized it was the first time she'd been off her feet since breakfast. During lunch, she'd been too busy to sit for more than a few seconds.

She wanted to make her guests comfortable, so she began talking about her impressions of Paradise Springs. While they asked questions in return, she waited for the opportunity to tell them about the odd situation with the twins. She avoided speaking of Isaiah other than to express how concerned he was about the youngsters. And she didn't mention Orpha Mast's call.

Reuben asked where she lived, and she told him. He smiled. "I know your bishop well, and we often meet on a Saturday halfway between his districts and mine for a cup of *kaffi*. If you've got a message you want to get to your family quickly, let me know, and I'll pass it along."

"Danki."

"If you can trust me with a letter, you can trust me with what's troubling you."

Clara wasn't surprised the bishop had guessed at her uneasiness by how she prattled like Andrew one minute and was almost as silent as Ammon the next. Setting her empty glass on the floor by her feet, she folded her hands in her lap.

"Isaiah and I," she said, "are concerned because the

twins tell us someone told them not to laugh. We're assuming it happened during the funeral."

"They don't laugh?" Wanda's eyes grew round as dismay lengthened her face.

She shook her head. "When I laughed, they were distressed until they decided the order wasn't for me. Just for them. But Isaiah and I've been trying not to laugh when they can hear."

Reuben began, "But they didn't react when I...?"

Wanda reached across the space between them and patted his hand. "Reuben, I've told you more than once you sound like an old mule braying. They probably weren't sure if that sound was a laugh." Looking back at Clara, she said, "Let me think and pray on this. There has to be something we can do."

Clara nodded but said nothing more about the problem. Instead, she welcomed the *kinder* onto the porch for more cookies and cool water. It was *gut* to see Isaiah had been right when he said the people of Paradise Springs were nice. She hoped so. She didn't want to meet more like his sister-in-law.

Dear Lord, help me find the words to explain to Orpha I'm the last person she needs to worry about interfering with her plans to marry Isaiah. She meant the prayer with all her heart.

Chapter Five

Isaiah arrived home in time to see his *mamm* and Reuben getting into their buggy. From where Clara stood, she could hear him talking to them. He was pleased they'd come to check on her and the *kinder*. He gave her a wave before he went into the barn to do chores. She hoped he didn't hurry, because she needed extra time to prepare their dinner after having company that afternoon.

When he came into the house after changing his clothes and his hair damp and smelling of strong soap, no remnants of smoke from his forge arrived with him. She appreciated that, because the odor would be tough to get out of the house.

"Wow! The chicken and parsley smell gōod," he said as he put his straw hat on the peg by the door.

"Perfect timing," she replied. The *kinder* were in their seats, because they'd been watching out the window to see when he emerged from the barn.

Isaiah reached the table as Clara put two plates containing freshly baked baking powder biscuits topped with gravy mixed with chunks of chicken in front of the girls. She gave him a smile before going to collect the boys' meals. On the table were bowls of cranberry sauce and corn.

As she placed a plate with three biscuits and chicken gravy in front of him, Clara said, "Don't worry. I saved a couple of your *mamm*'s cookies for you."

"More cookies?" asked Andrew, his eyes lighting up.

"Once we eat our dinner." She added as the twins reached for their forks, "And we'll eat after Isaiah leads us in saying grace."

Waiting until Clara had served herself and was sitting with the girls, Isaiah bowed his head. Again she watched the youngsters do the same, and grief pulsed through her. Their parents had taught their *kinder* to be grateful to God. She hoped Isaiah would make sure they didn't forget those lessons.

With the first bite he took, Isaiah turned to her with an astounded look. "This is amazing. You had only a few minutes to prepare the meal."

"It's a quick one."

"These biscuits are so light they would float away if they weren't weighed down with the chicken and gravy."

"Danki." She hoped her face wasn't red at his compliment. She shouldn't take pleasure in his praise, but she couldn't remember the last time anyone had complimented her cooking.

"Did you enjoy *Mamm*'s and Reuben's visit?" Isaiah asked once he'd cleaned his plate.

"We did." Clara smiled as she placed a cookie beside each *kind*'s plate. "They're an adorable couple." She set the last two cookies in front of him.

Again he regarded her with astonishment. "My *mamm* and the bishop aren't a couple. Just *gut* friends who have known each other for years."

"Are you sure?" She took her seat again and picked up her cookie. Her smile broadened as she took a delicate bite.

"Very sure. Don't start playing the matchmaker, too."

"No, no." She shook her head. "I don't have any interest in that. I was remarking on what my eyes showed me."

He paused, not answering for a long minute. When he did, incredulity remained in his voice. "I want to say your eyes are mistaken, but I can't help thinking of the number of times *Mamm* and Reuben have been in each other's company the past six or eight months. Reuben has joined us for dinner at least a couple of times each month, and I've seen her talking with him on church Sundays while the two of them walked alone together. I guess I should take a closer look myself next time."

Clara was grateful when Andrew started talking about what the *kinder* had done that day. Isaiah must have been, too, because he listened and asked questions and kept the twins chattering about their games and their chores and how Clara had taught them a fun way to bring their dirty laundry downstairs while they sang a silly song.

A quick glance told her he was well aware of what he was doing, but she didn't attempt to turn the conversation to the subject of his *mamm* and Reuben. Probably he wanted to avoid talking about anything to do with matchmaking, too.

As far as she was concerned, that was the best plan ever!

When, after dinner, Clara had the twins help her clear the table and do the dishes, Isaiah went out to do the last of the chores. He'd noticed his buggy horse, Chocolate Chip—or Chip for short—had been favoring his front right leg on the way home. A quick check showed no signs of damage, but he wondered if the horse had strained the leg. Perhaps Clara would be willing for him to use her Bella tomorrow.

His mind was reeling about Clara's comments about *Mamm* and Reuben. What if Clara was right? How could he have failed to notice his *mamm*'s interest in Reuben? They'd lost their spouses at least five years ago. He almost groaned aloud. If Reuben married *Mamm*, the pressure would increase for Isaiah to find another wife. On the other hand, he wished the bishop and his *mamm* every happiness, so maybe he could find a way to turn Marlin's attention from Isaiah to the fact their bishop was getting remarried. No, Marlin was like a hound dog with a scent. He wasn't going to let up until after Isaiah's wedding supper.

Isaiah walked from the stable to the house, hurrying to put his thoughts behind him. When he came inside, he saw the *kinder* had gathered around Clara, who sat on the rocking chair. Andrew leaned his elbow on the arm and watched what she was doing. The others stretched out on the floor with their coloring books.

As he came into the living room, Andrew grinned at him. "Guess what, *Onkel* Isaiah?"

"What, kiddo?" he asked, as he did each time one of the twins asked him that question.

"We're writing to *Aenti* Debra," crowed Andrew. "Next we're gonna write to *Grossdawdi* and *Grossmammi*."

"Here's my picture," said Nancy, holding up a page she'd torn from her coloring book. She edged around him and held it out to Clara. "Give to *Aenti* Debra? She see how *gut* I color."

Clara smiled. "You asked first, so you can put your picture in to your *aenti*. Nettie Mae, why don't you color one for your grandparents? Then tomorrow night, it'll be the boys' turn. That way, it'll be easy to keep track of whose turn it is each day."

"You're writing to their grandparents?" Isaiah asked, shocked.

"I will be," she said without looking up again or pausing as she filled the page with her neat penmanship. "After I finish this letter to their *aenti*. I found their addresses in a book in a kitchen drawer, and the twins were willing to share stories about their day." She smiled at them before raising her eyes toward him.

Her smile faded, and he knew he'd failed to keep his thoughts hidden. When she asked what was wrong, he didn't answer. Instead, he asked a question of his own. "Can we talk about this after they're in bed?"

She nodded, and he saw her bafflement. He couldn't blame her. His voice had been sharper than he'd intended, but to apologize in front of the *kinder* was guaranteed to bring question after question from them. He couldn't explain to them when he wasn't able to explain to himself why seeing Clara write the letter bothered him.

But his request put a damper on the twins' excitement. Their voices were subdued, and they glanced uneasily at him while Clara wrote to their grandparents. She promised she would take the *kinder* to the post office tomorrow to buy stamps and send the letters.

"I'd be glad to do that," Isaiah said, as she put the letters on the table beside her chair.

"We can do it." Her voice was prim and cool. "I know how pressured you are to get your job completed."

"True." Why did he sense that a scold underlined her

sympathetic words? Maybe because his old companion—guilt—was rearing its head again. How many times had he said the wrong thing and upset Rose? For a man who'd been ordained as a minister and who should know the weight words possessed, he spoke too many times without considering which ones he chose.

When he asked if he could use her horse tomorrow, she agreed and didn't ask why he needed Bella. Instead, she herded the *kinder* upstairs. He followed, feeling like an outsider in the house he'd considered as much his home as his less than a mile down the road.

Isaiah went back downstairs as soon as the kids were tucked in their beds. He'd seen the glances they aimed at him and Clara. They sensed the wall she'd thrown up in the wake of his unthinking question.

Going outside to get a breath of fresh air, he glanced at the sky. He'd been sticking his foot in his mouth a lot lately. Was it because he'd put distance between him and God since Rose's death? He'd guarded his prayers as he'd tried to figure out why a loving Father would let his wife die alone. Couldn't God have given him a hint to stay home that day? What other mistakes was Isaiah going to make as he bumbled forward?

He didn't know, and he didn't want to guess.

The door opened behind him, and Clara stepped onto the porch. The moonlight washed out her ginger hair, but his mind recreated the vibrant color. He shouldn't be thinking about how pretty she was, but he couldn't deny what his eyes showed him.

"I thought you might like something cool to drink." She held out a glass to him. When he took it and peered into the glass, trying to figure out its contents, she added, "It's ice tea."

She sat on the glider, right in the middle, in an unspoken warning she didn't want him beside her. He often sat on it because he liked its easy motion, but a glance at the road passing by the house warned him that anyone driving by would have a clear view of the porch. Besides, he couldn't blame her for making it clear she was perturbed with him.

Leaning against the rail, he stared across the yard. If she were only perturbed, he'd be relieved.

"What's bothering you, Isaiah?" she asked when he remained silent.

"I assumed you'd talk to me before you made any decisions for the *kinder*." As soon as the words left his lips, he realized how petty they sounded.

"I will if that's what you want." Her voice became as icy as the cubes in his tea. "But you hired me to take care of them. I can't do that if I have to wait to talk to you about everything."

He grimaced. "I know. Forget I said that."

"What's bothering you, Isaiah?" she asked again. "What's *really* bothering you?"

"If I tell you I don't know, please don't think I'm trying to be evasive." He sighed. "I'd like to blame it on stress."

"Why don't we?" She gave him a faint smile. "We're trying to help the twins, and there are bound to be times when we rub each other the wrong way."

"I appreciate it." He did. She could have quit; then what would he have done? Finding someone else and disrupting the *kinder* who were already close to her would be difficult. Unless he asked Orpha, and he didn't want *that* trouble. "Why don't you tell me about these letters you and the twins were writing?"

"They are a sort of circle letter with their family. From

what they told me earlier, they don't know any of them well, and I doubt their *aenti* and grandparents know much about them. This way, they can get acquainted so when the *kinder* go to live with whomever will be taking them, they won't feel as if they're living with strangers."

He was astonished at her foresight. He'd been busy trying to get through each day, dealing with his sorrow and trying not to upset the grieving *kinder*. He hadn't given the future much thought. Or maybe he didn't want to admit that one day soon the youngsters would leave Paradise Springs. His last connection to his best friend would be severed. No doubt, the twins would stay in contact with him at Christmas or maybe on their birthdays, but he wasn't sure if he'd ever see them again once they moved to California or Florida or the *gut* Lord knew where with their family.

The thought pierced his heart, and he turned and put his hands on the porch railing as his stomach twisted. The moon was rising, its cool light unable to ease the hot pain within him. His hands tightened on the wood, driving chips of paint into his palms.

Clara said, "If you'd rather I didn't send out the letters—"

"Send them," he interrupted and saw shock widening her eyes. "I'm sorry. I didn't mean to sound upset."

"But you are."

He nodded. "Upset and guilty."

"Don't feel guilty you have to work and can't spend every minute with them." She gave him another whisper of a smile. "I don't spend every minute with them, though I don't let them out of my sight. They're young, and they don't want to be shadowed by an adult."

"Everything you say makes sense."

"But?"

"I can't help believing that I'm shunting my responsibilities off on someone else."

"Esta must have used a babysitter sometimes. The *kinder* didn't go to the auction with her and Melvin."

"Thank the *gut* Lord they didn't." He let his sigh sift through his clenched teeth. "Like I said, everything you're saying makes sense, but I want to make sure Melvin's faith in me as a substitute *daed* wasn't misplaced. The twins deserve a *gut daed*, but all they have is me."

"You're doing fine under the circumstances."

"You mean when the funeral was such a short time ago?"

"No, I mean when every single woman in the district is determined to be your next wife, and your deacon is egging them on."

In spite of himself, Isaiah chuckled quietly. He didn't want the sound of his laughter to reach the *kinder* upstairs. Clara's teasing was exactly what he needed. Her comments put the silliness into perspective. If he could remember that the next time Marlin or someone else brought up the topic of him marrying, maybe he could stop making a mess of everything. He hoped so.

Chapter Six

$\curvearrowleft$

As he reentered the front room of his brother Joshua's house where the worship service was already underway, Isaiah tried to convince himself this day was like every other church Sunday since he'd become one of the district's two ministers. Earlier, he'd greeted the members of the *Leit* as they gathered outside the barn before the worship service started. The men entered, followed by the women, both accompanied by the younger *kinder*. Next came the older girls with unmarried women. At the end were the unmarried men and the boys who no longer had to sit with their parents. While the *Leit* began the first hymn, he'd joined Reuben, Marlin and Atlee in a separate room to pray and plan the three-hour-long service. Isaiah was chosen to give the first sermon, the shorter one that lasted about a half hour.

Exactly like many other church Sundays since he was ordained.

But nothing was as it'd been before.

The Beachy twins were with Clara instead of their parents, and he wouldn't be able to look over at the men's side and see his best friend, who'd been encouraging when Isaiah was first chosen as a minister. Melvin had listened while Isaiah poured out his worries with his Rose's dismay at having the lot fall on him.

Dear Rose. As fragile as the blossoms of the flower that shared her name. She'd come to see the selection as part of the path God had set out for them.

Far better than Isaiah had accepted her death as God's will. He didn't understand how God could take Rose when everything was beginning to go well for them. Every way he looked at it told him submitting to God's will was the sole way to comprehend what had happened. It should be simple for him, as a minister in their district, to take the path laid out in front of him. It should be, but it wasn't.

When *Das Loblied*, their second hymn, was finished, Isaiah didn't sit like the rest of the worshippers. He moved to the front and greeted the congregation before he began to speak. The thoughts he'd organized during the long, slow singing of the hymn tumbled out of his head when his gaze collided with Clara's. Somehow, in the past hour, he'd forgotten how remarkable her brown eyes were. They were filled with anticipation for what he was about to say.

He opened his mouth, ready to give voice to his thoughts, but what came out was, "I—I—I…th-that is, I—I—I wa-wa-wanted to s-s-say…"

Astonishment filled the faces looking at him, but nobody was more surprised than he was. Not once, not even the first time when he'd stood to give a sermon after the lot fell upon him, had he stuttered over his opening words. Each time, he'd easily shared his faith with those who sat in front of him.

Shock raced through him. Had inspiration left him

because he'd been fighting the path God had set out before him? Or was it something far simpler—and far more complicated at the same time? Was it because Clara Ebersol sat among the women?

He glanced at her as he struggled to fight off panic. When her gaze met his, she gave him a half smile and a slight nod before her eyes led his to the twins sitting on either side of her. They were watching him with eager expressions. What could he say that would touch their hearts as well as the adults'?

For a moment, he almost asked God for help but halted himself. Until he was willing to accept the Lord's plan for him, he shouldn't ask. Instead, he gathered the sight of Clara and the *kinder* close. A sense of calm settled over him like a warm blanket on a wintry night. He couldn't let his grief keep him from helping Melvin's boys and girls. With that thought to guide him, he started, speaking of *kinder* and how blessed those were who loved them and were given the sacred duty of raising them to know and love God. Later, when he'd resumed his place with Reuben and Atlee, he couldn't recall a word of what he'd said, but several women had tears running down their cheeks. A few men were dabbing at their cheeks with white handkerchiefs. He'd spoken from the heart, and he'd touched theirs. Not him. It'd been the word of God coming through him.

Bowing his head, he praised God for using him as a conduit when Isaiah was resisting God's will. And he thanked the Lord for sending Clara as an inspiration. He couldn't ignore the fact that her being at the service had helped to shape his words in a way nothing had since his mourning began. Not only her presence, but what he'd observed for the past week while she'd worked to keep the Beachy *kinder* happy and prevent them from falling into the chasm of grief he knew too well.

The rest of the three-hour-long service passed so quickly he was startled. After singing the closing hymn in the slow unison style of their tradition, he watched the congregation exit, the youngest first. He walked out with the men and smiled at those who smiled in his direction. Nobody would tell him he'd done a *gut* job. A preacher must never have too much pride.

"Isaiah!"

At the call of his name, Isaiah tensed and turned to face the members of the Mast family, who were closing in on him like a pack of coydogs ready to pounce on a rooster. Curtis Mast, a man shaped like a bull with massive shoulders, led the way.

Isaiah dreaded this part of Sunday. His late wife's parents didn't seem to care if they were in the midst of the rest of the *Leit* when they cornered him. They found a way to remind him that they believed he should be married, and marrying another of their other daughters would be the best solution.

"*Gute mariye*, Curtis," he said to Rose's *daed*. Looking at her *mamm*, a slight woman who was as pretty as her four surviving daughters who followed behind them, he added, "*Gute mariye*, Ida Mae."

For a moment, when they nodded in his direction, he thought they'd walk right past him without matchmaking, in spite of calling out to him. Instead, they stopped and stared at him. He fought not to squirm under their regard. He wasn't a *kind* who'd gotten caught trying to steal a few extra cookies. He was a man suffering the same grief they did.

"An interesting topic for your sermon today," Curtis

said as if they'd already been chatting. It was like Curtis to get to the point. He had opinions, and he shared them. Too readily, some people said, but Isaiah appreciated knowing where he stood with his father-in-law. Except on the remarrying issue!

"Ja," added his wife, "a man who has no *kinder* preaching to those of us who do." Her voice cracked as she added, "And to those who have lost a precious *kind*."

"Don't be silly, Ida Mae," Rose's *daed* added with a narrow-eyed frown at his wife. "Isaiah is gaining a lot of experience. Don't forget. He's a temporary *daed* at the moment." He gave Isaiah a companionable elbow in the side. *"Gut* practice for when you have *kinder* of your own. My girls love *kinder*, don't you, girls?"

Orpha twittered a soft laugh. *"Ja.* Love them." She edged closer to him. "I can't wait to have a family. That's every Amish girl's dream, ain't so?"

Isaiah kept his sigh silent. He'd tried everything to persuade Rose's parents and her sisters that he'd marry again when the time—and the woman—was right. He'd tried agreeing with them to put an end to these conversations, but that made them more persistent about him courting Orpha or one of the other girls. Curtis and Ida Mae didn't seem to care which he married as long as it was one of their daughters. He'd tried being honest with them, but they'd acted as if they didn't hear a single word he said.

"Ja," came a voice from behind him. "And perhaps that's why Isaiah's sermon this morning was interesting." Clara stepped forward and smiled at the whole Mast family. "I'm Clara Ebersol. I don't think we've met."

He was relieved she'd halted the Masts before they could say something else to twist his arm into proposing to Orpha right on his brother's lawn. *Judge not, and ye shall not be judged: condemn not, and ye shall not be condemned: forgive, and ye shall be forgiven.* How many times had he repeated that verse from Luke in his mind to remind himself the Masts were grieving, too?

Then he realized how he'd misjudged the abrupt silence after Clara introduced herself to the family. A silent message he couldn't read passed between the members of the Mast family, and then six pairs of eyes riveted on Clara. They saw her as an unwanted intruder, competition in their determination to have him marry a Mast girl. He resisted the instinct to step between her and them. Why would they see this as a contest with a proposal from him as the trophy? He was no prize as a husband.

"*You* are Clara Ebersol?" asked Ida Mae with unconcealed dismay. Turning to her oldest, she said, "You didn't say she was a redhead."

Isaiah had no idea why the color of Clara's hair mattered to Ida Mae. He said nothing while the Masts introduced themselves to Clara with tight smiles. Holding his breath, he waited for what they might say next.

Clara ignored the glowers aimed at her by Orpha and her younger sisters. Instead, she spoke warmly with the Masts, talking about the Beachy twins as if his in-laws had asked about them. When she told a story of the boys' latest escapade that had left them covered with mud, she laughed without a hint of anything but amusement.

The Masts laughed with her, though it sounded strained in Isaiah's ears. Maybe he was too sensitive, looking for trouble where none existed. Just because Orpha had been cold to Clara the other morning wasn't any reason to believe the rest of her family wished anyone ill.

Turning to him, Clara said, "Reuben has been looking

for you, Isaiah. I told him I'd deliver the message." As she motioned him to follow her, she paused and looked at the dumbfounded Masts. "It's been nice to meet you. I look forward to getting to know you better during my time here."

Isaiah went with her. His farewell to the Masts wasn't returned. They looked stunned by Clara's sunny smile and kindness. He wondered how long ago it'd been since anyone in the district had spoken with warmth and hope to them instead of focusing on their grief.

As others did to him.

Sympathy surged through him. He needed to reconsider how he talked to them next time he encountered them. He would pray for God's guidance in finding the right words to rebuild the bridge that had collapsed with Rose's death. It was his duty as their minister and their son-in-law to help them—and himself—to climb out of the deep, dark pit of grief.

He hoped there was a way, other than proposing to one of their daughters, for them to heed him.

"So that's the Mast family," Clara said as she walked with Isaiah around the far side of the house. "Your in-laws."

"Ja." He didn't say anything more.

She started to speak, then thought better of it. Isaiah was stressed enough already. He didn't need her warnings that Orpha wasn't the only one who wanted him remarried to a Mast girl. At least two of the other three had given her ill-concealed scowls. Instead, she asked, "How are you?"

His mouth worked, then he spat in candid frustration, "Could they be any more obvious?"

She couldn't keep from smiling. "Don't you think it's better the matchmakers are obvious rather than sneaky?"

"Better maybe, but not easier." He looked at her with a sheepish grin. "I'm sorry, Clara. I know none of this matchmaking was what you expected when you took this job."

"I didn't. That's why I'm extra grateful you were honest with me right from the beginning about the district's matchmakers." She grinned. "Though I have to admit I already had a very *gut* idea of what was on Orpha's mind when she stopped by the first morning I was here."

"I wish the Masts would show as much common sense as you do."

"Did you consider they care about you enough that they want to keep you as a son-in-law and having you marry one of their daughters would be the best way to ensure that?"

He halted and stared at her as if she'd announced a cow had jumped over the moon. She almost laughed at the thought. Spending time with young *kinder* was leaving her with nursery rhymes on the brain. She pushed the silly thoughts aside. Her question had stunned him, and she wondered why he'd never considered the idea before.

"You have a kindhearted way of looking at people," Isaiah said as they came around the corner of the house and saw Reuben talking with two men by the clothesline. "Sometimes it's easier to give into suspicion."

"Suspicion leads to making me think I'm different from others. That way can lead to *hochmut*." She lowered her eyes and shut her lips before she could say more.

Her *daed* lectured her often on the sin of *hochmut*, but he was the proudest person she knew. When she was younger, she hadn't understood his resolve for them to look like the perfect family around other families in their district. Even making a single mistake would reflect poorly on the family and on him. To be jilted by a young man her *daed* had bragged about marrying his daughter was the worst thing she could have done, in *Daed*'s estimation.

She was glad when Isaiah excused himself and went to speak with the bishop. As unsettled as thoughts of her *daed* and of Lonnie made her, she'd be wise to keep silent.

Clara collected the Beachy twins, who were playing with the other youngsters, and made sure they got something to eat after the men had finished with the midday meal. She didn't have to worry about them being finicky, though she noticed Nettie Mae holding her fork at a strange angle once or twice and examining the food before she popped it into her mouth.

As soon as they were finished, she joined other women in the kitchen washing up. The twins went to play tag with *kinder* their ages, and Clara kept an eye on them out the kitchen window.

She emerged from the kitchen with the women who'd welcomed her as if they'd known her all their lives to see Isaiah walking toward her. She heard whispers behind her, but she paid them no attention as he asked where the *kinder* were.

"Over there." She pointed to where they were running away from a little girl who was It. "Are you ready to head home?"

"Not yet." He glanced past her at the other women as he added, "Just trying to keep track of them."

"You don't need to worry," said an older woman whose name Clara remembered was Fannie Beiler. "Your Clara has been checking on them every minute."

Isaiah struggled not to react to Fannie calling her "your Clara." She wanted to reassure him that Fannie meant nothing by her words. It was just a way of speaking.

"Let me know when you're ready to leave," Clara said quickly. "I'll have the twins ready to go."

"Danki." He glanced past her with abrupt puzzlement. "Odd."

She looked over her shoulder and saw the other women had moved away.

"Not odd. They're being nice to allow us time to discuss the *kinder.*"

"Or whatever we might have on our minds."

Refusing to let him bring up the subject of matchmaking again, because this time she believed he was mistaken, she said, "Fannie Beiler has been very welcoming to me."

"Fannie is my older brother Ezra's mother-in-law. She's not interested in matchmaking, but it seems to be everywhere."

"Ignore it. If your friends see you bothered by their comments, they're sure to tease you more."

"True, especially my brothers."

Annoyed the subject had once again turned to matchmaking, she wished they could talk of something else. The topic seemed to make her notice how *gut*-looking Isaiah was, and her mind wandered to wondering about having him take her home in his courting buggy. Just the two of them without the twins tossing question after question from the rear of the family buggy.

"How is Reuben?" she asked, grasping on to the first thought she had of something other than walking out with Isaiah. "He appeared on edge when he asked me to find you."

"He's worried about his oldest. Katie Kay has been pushing the limits of our *Ordnung* for over a year."

"It isn't easy to be in a bishop's family and be held up to be a role model for everyone in two districts. The son of my bishop went out and bought himself a sporty car and parked it right in front of his family's house for a few months." She hesitated, then said, "If the Beachy *kinder* were a bit older, they'd find themselves put into that position, too, because you're one of the ministers."

"I'm glad they aren't older. They have enough to distress them."

Again Clara hesitated, but she couldn't keep her concerns silent any longer. "I wish they would act more distressed. They seem to take their parents' deaths in stride during the day. At night, it's a whole other thing, because every night one or the other of them has a nightmare. Sometimes more than one. Don't you think they should be showing more grief?"

"We each show grief in a unique way."

"Don't try to placate me with platitudes, Isaiah. I'm not saying this to you because you're their minister. I'm saying this to you because you're the only *daed* they have. Doesn't it bother you, too?"

"It does, but I can't bring myself to do anything that would make them more unhappy."

Clara gave him a sad smile and reached out to pat his arm. The moment her fingers brushed the skin below his shirtsleeve, a flurry of sensation sped through her like a fiery storm wind. His gaze darted toward her, and she saw his astonishment as well. Astonishment and more, as deeper, stronger emotions burned in the depths of his eyes. She should move her fingers, but they seemed soldered to his arm by the strength of the feelings she couldn't name because they changed like a kaleidoscope being twirled at top speed.

Did he murmur her name? She couldn't tell because her heart was setting off explosion after explosion inside her. When his fingers slid atop hers, the warmth of his skin above her hand and below was more *wunderbaar* than anything she'd experienced before. But how could that be?

She'd had her hand held before. She'd been kissed before, but nothing had overwhelmed her like this. When Lonnie—

The thought of her ex-fiancé's name broke the hold Isaiah had over her. It was as if she'd stepped from a heated kitchen into a predawn winter freeze. With a shiver, she yanked her hand away. She had let her emotions run away with her.

Again.

She was making foolish decisions.

Again.

Before Clara could come up with an excuse that would allow her to walk away without insulting him, she heard, "Isaiah! Clara! *Komm* and sit with us!"

She looked across the yard to where two people sat on a bench facing Wanda Stoltzfus, who was rocking on the front porch. The man, though his hair was a few shades darker, looked enough like Isaiah that she guessed the two men must be related. Beside him sat a pretty blonde. His arm was stretched across the back of the bench behind her in a rare suggestion of intimacy among the plain folk. Was she his wife? No courting couple would be that obvious about the affection between them.

Her conjecture was confirmed when Isaiah introduced the two as his older brother Ezra and Ezra's wife, Leah. As she greeted them, she was relieved nobody mentioned her and Isaiah standing together.

Isaiah brought two lawn chairs onto the porch so they could sit and chat. He gave her a glance she guessed was intended to tell her something. He was wasting his time. She was so discombobulated she had to focus on acting normal.

Within a few minutes, the uneasiness ebbed, and Clara was drawn into a conversation with Isaiah's sister-in-law. Clara enjoyed Leah's enthusiastic discussion of the best fabrics for quilting. Clara wasn't surprised to hear Leah's quilts were prized by *Englisch* tourists who stopped at the family's grocery store. Wanda told her that they sold as soon as they were placed on display.

Clara looked again and again at the twins to make sure they were all right, and she listened to the conversations swirling around her as the Stoltzfus family talked about their plans for the upcoming week. It was as she'd imagined a loving family would be.

Too bad she'd be in Paradise Springs for only a month or so. Once the twins' grandparents or *aenti* came to collect them, she would have to return home. A sigh of regret surged through her because, though she could take with her *wunderbaar* memories of the Stoltzfus family and the Beachy twins, she had to wonder if knowing how families *could* be would make it more difficult to live with her exacting *daed*.

Chapter Seven

Clara draped the wet dish towel over the rack connected to the cabinet. She adjusted the arm so any drips fell into the sink. While she listened to water go down the drain, she gazed out the window over the sink and smiled. It felt *gut* to smile as she'd been up most of the night with the twins as one after another was caught in the throes of a nightmare. They couldn't tell her what scared them, but she suspected the bad dreams were caused by the grief they refused to speak about during the day. Every night, one or more of them woke her and each other with shrieks of terror. It had become a ritual in the morning for Isaiah to ask who had managed to sleep through the night. He'd offered to trade off with her and tend to them at night, but she reminded him that he'd hired her because he couldn't be with the twins night and day.

Otherwise each day unfolded into the next. In the past four days, the weather had been splendid. The *kinder* preferred to be outside, and she'd smiled at their cheers when she told them they didn't have to wear shoes any longer. She'd removed hers for working in the house and the yard. The grass was silken soft, and, when she checked out the vegetable plants growing among the weeds in the garden, the cool, damp earth had been delightful between her toes.

Each day, she worked on the garden. She guessed Esta had kept the garden neat, but in the three weeks since her death, nobody had spent time on the garden. The early peas were ready to harvest, or they would have been if not choked by weeds. She'd spent the morning pulling weeds before the twins' noon meal.

Now they were fed and playing in the sandbox beneath the large maple. She wanted to give them time to tire themselves out more before their naps. She was surprised when the older twins fell asleep every afternoon, but guessed they were exhausted from night terrors and other bad dreams. The boys pushed trucks and tractors around, making roads and furrows in the sand. Both girls shoveled sand into a pail and tipped it over to build temporary mountains for the boys' vehicles. As the sand sifted down the piles, they scooped it up and started over again.

Her one attempt this week to discuss their parents with them had been useless. She'd asked what was their favorite meal made by their *mamm*. A simple question, but none of them answered. Instead, they edged closer together as they had when she and Isaiah asked about why they wouldn't laugh. They'd watched her with guarded expressions until she urged them to go out and play.

What else had been said to them other than not to laugh? They'd taken her urging to sing quietly to heart, so had someone else told them not to talk about their parents? That made no sense, but neither did telling youngsters who were mourning their *mamm* and *daed* to stop laughing.

She needed to talk to Isaiah. Maybe tonight. For now, with the twins busy, she should check the answering machine in the phone shack. Isaiah had mentioned that morning at breakfast how it needed to be done, and she'd offered to do it. She'd wondered if he'd be as annoyed as he'd been about the letter writing last week, but he nodded with a grateful smile.

Each evening, he arrived home wiped out from his long hours of working at his forge. He hadn't said much, but even the youngsters knew his important job needed to be done by the week's end. He'd skipped breakfast the past two days, and she wondered how much he ate while he pushed to finish his project. At dinner, he barely kept his eyes open and didn't eat much. Even the chicken and biscuits he'd raved about hadn't convinced him to do more than pick at his food.

Clara put on her black bonnet before, with a final glance at the youngsters, she went out the front door. Though she was worried Isaiah was trying to do too much, she couldn't nag him. He was her employer. If she were sent home early, her *daed* would believe she'd shamed her family again.

"And in this case, it'd be true," she said as she crossed the yard to the farm lane that ran as straight as a ruler between the house and the road.

But she was worrying unnecessarily. Isaiah needed her at the house. Otherwise, he wouldn't finish his commission on time. She wondered what he was creating. He never spoke of the project other than he must have it done before the arrival of the truck taking it to Maryland.

If he didn't go into the *dawdi haus* as soon as the *kinder* were in bed each night, she might have had the opportunity to ask about what he was making. Tonight, she must speak with him about how to reach the youngsters and urge them to mourn as they should.

At the end of the lane, the phone shack looked like an abandoned outhouse, stuck as it was out by the mailbox. Clara opened the door. Her nose wrinkled at the smell of air cooped up too long. The small building held an uncomfortable bench and a counter stuck in a corner. The single window allowed in light, but was shut tight and edged with spiderwebs littered with white egg sacs. A dusty phone sat on the counter between an answering machine and pencil and a notepad. A list of numbers in a plastic sleeve had been nailed to the wall. They were for the local medical clinic, as well as other phone numbers that might be needed in an emergency.

She wasn't surprised to see the answering machine blinking. When had it last been checked?

Picking up the pencil, she shifted the notepad so she could write any messages. She wasn't sure if the Beachys were the only family who used the phone shack or if it was shared with Amish neighbors. If the latter, she'd deliver any messages right away.

Clara pushed the blinking red light, and a disembodied voice announced there were five messages on the machine. The first was a hang-up, and the second had a message of, "Sorry. Wrong number." She deleted both.

The third call was different. A woman said in a pleasant voice, "Good afternoon. I'm calling from Paradise Springs Optical, and this message is for Esta Beachy. Esta, the glasses you ordered for Nettie Mae are in. We look forward to seeing you at your earliest convenience."

She let the rest of the message play. Blinking back tears, she was glad she hadn't brought the *kinder* with her. To hear the message meant for their *mamm* would have upset them. Look how it was distressing her, and she'd never met Esta Beachy.

But in a way she had. She'd met Esta and Melvin through their twins, who were bright and curious and helpful and loving. The couple had been training up their family well. She recalled the proverb she'd often heard *Mamm* repeat: *Train up a child in the way he should go: and when he is old, he will not depart from it.* The Beachys had started their youngsters off on the right foot.

Listening to the message again, she wrote down the phone number the caller had left. She listened to the final two calls, but both were for political candidates. Those she deleted before she made a call to confirm the glasses ordered for Nettie Mae were still at the shop.

The woman who answered at the shop expressed her sympathy for what the Beachy family had suffered before confirming that the glasses were waiting for Nettie Mae to have them fitted. She gave Clara the address and the times the store was open.

"I'll bring her in later this afternoon," Clara said before thanking the woman and ending the call.

At least once a day, Isaiah mentioned something about how he and Melvin had been best friends and how often he'd joined the family for the evening meal. He must have known about the little girl's eye exam. Why hadn't he mentioned anything to her about Nettie Mae getting glasses?

No matter, she knew now.

Hurrying to the sandbox, she asked the twins if they wanted to go to town with her. When they scrambled out of the box, she smiled and motioned for them to shake sand off their clothes. She brushed as much out of their hair as she could. There wasn't time to give them baths before they drove into Paradise Springs.

The twins ran into the house to collect their shoes. She followed and pulled on her black sneakers before she went into the stable next to the barn to hitch Bella to the Beachys' family buggy. It was less cramped than hers.

Once shoes were on the correct feet and tied, she watched the youngsters climb into the buggy. The boys again chose the back, and the two girls sat on the front seat. Checking the house was secure and she hadn't left anything on, she got in.

"Let's go, Bella," she called.

The *kinder* copied her words, and the horse tilted her head as if wondering why she was getting the same command from different people.

The twins pelted Clara with questions. Where were they going? Who would they see? What would they do? When would they get home? Could they order pizza to bring home for dinner?

She faltered on the last question. She doubted she had enough money in her purse to pay for pizza for the six of them.

"Oh, dear!" she gasped.

Eyeglasses would be far more expensive than two large pizzas. She'd never given any thought to how the glasses would be paid for. Seeing the sign for the Stoltzfus Family Shops ahead, she turned Bella into the parking lot. She drew in the horse when a man waved to her from the general store.

She recognized him as Isaiah's brother Amos. He had reddish-brown hair, but he and Isaiah had the same shaped face and height. As she stopped in front of him, she saw Amos's hands, like Isaiah's, showed he was accustomed to hard work.

Greeting her, he smiled and asked what she and the *kinder* were up to.

"We've got errands to run this afternoon," she replied, "but I need to check a couple of things with Isaiah first."

Amos smiled at the twins. "Why don't I take them in the store while you two talk?"

"They can be boisterous."

"Don't worry. I'm accustomed to little ones." Waving his hand, he said, "C'mon, kids." As they poured out of the buggy, he added, "Let's see what *Onkel* Amos can find for you in the store." He led them like the Pied Piper into his shop.

Clara smiled. *Onkel* Amos? No wonder Melvin had asked Isaiah to be the guardian of his *kinder*. The whole Stoltzfus family welcomed her and the Beachy twins. She was never going to take a moment of her time with them for granted.

Isaiah looked up in surprise when a familiar silhouette walked toward his smithy. What was Clara doing here at this hour? And where were the twins?

She paused in the doorway as she'd done the first time and said as if he'd asked his second question aloud, "The *kinder* are with Amos. He offered to let them pick out a treat."

"He loves doing that for all his nieces and nephews. He makes sure he has plenty of ice cream and candy for them to choose from." He lowered the hammer he'd been using to pound the heated metal thin enough so he could twist it. "Are you in town for something specific?"

She explained the message from the optician on the answering machine. "I'll try to check it more often."

"I didn't know Nettie Mae had been taken to be examined for glasses," he said. He'd thought it would be simple for him to step in as surrogate *daed* until the *kinder*'s family returned. How silly that seemed now!

He was relieved Clara had taken over disciplining the *kinder*. He'd been the fun *onkel*, the one who played with them and tickled them and taught them how to do fun things like skip stones and feed chickens. To become their *daed* and raise them to be *gut* members of their community was a completely different role, and he hadn't been prepared for the responsibilities.

"I'm sure the glasses are strong enough to put up with a three-year-old's antics," Clara said, and he realized she'd misunderstood his silence. One of the few times that had happened.

He latched on to her change of subject as if it were a lifeline. "Esta would have made sure. She wouldn't have wanted to bring the glasses in for repairs all the time. Too costly."

Color rose up Clara's cheeks, astonishing him until she said, "I should have asked if there was an unpaid balance for the glasses."

"Don't worry. What's owed is what's owed."

"I can't argue with that." She chuckled. "Oh, it feels *gut* to laugh."

"Any clues as to who told the kids not to laugh?"

"None," she replied sadly.

He wished he hadn't asked the question. He liked her laugh when she didn't have to restrain herself. It was genuine and hearty and invited him to join in.

"How much do you think glasses for a three-year-old cost?" he asked.

"My *mamm* complained about the high cost when she picked up hers a few months ago. They were almost four hundred dollars."

He grimaced. "I had no idea glasses were that expensive." He tapped the pair hanging around his neck. "My safety glasses cost between ten and twenty bucks, depending on what I buy. The face shield I use for welding is two or three times as much."

"The glasses my *mamm* got were bifocals, so I assume Nettie Mae's should be cheaper."

"Unless she needs bifocals."

Clara considered that, then shook her head. "I've noticed her getting very close and then pulling back when she's holding something or when she's coloring. But she seems to see fine at a distance. She was the first one to point out three deer in a field on our way here."

He went to a table and yanked a drawer open. Reaching in, he lifted out a checkbook. "What's the name of the optician?"

"Paradise Springs Optical... I think. I left the page with it at the house."

"That's okay." He shoved aside his apron and pulled out a pen. Scribbling his name at the bottom of the check, he tore it out of the book and handed it to her.

"You're giving me a blank check?"

He smiled. "I trust you with the twins, who are far more important to me than my bank account, so why wouldn't I trust you with a check?"

She was touched by his words. He wondered why. She should have realized the truth. No amount of money could recompense him if something happened to one of the *kinder*.

"*Danki,*" she said at last. She folded the check and put it in the black purse hanging over her right shoulder. Looking past him, she asked, "Are those what you need to get done before the week is out?"

"*Ja.*" He motioned for her to come closer to the great gates that were almost completed. They were more than twelve feet high and almost as wide, too big to fit in the shop.

As she stepped past him, he drew in a deep breath of the faint scent from her shampoo. It was out of place among the odors of heated metal and coal. Apple, if he wasn't mistaken. An aroma that suited her well because apples could be tart or sweet.

She gazed at the two gates. The arched tops were accented by twisted posts, leading the eye to the huge metal medallions in the center of each section.

"They're beautiful." She ran a finger along the medallion with the large *T* in the center. "Does this stand for something?"

"The first word in the name of my client's horse farm. Look at the other one. It has an *S* on it. Taggart Stables."

"These are stunning, Isaiah."

He turned away and set the rod he'd been working on into the fire. He shouldn't be pleased with her compliment. It was a challenge to be creative and not take pride in his work. The elegant gates weren't anything he'd want on his property, but he'd followed the design the *Englischer* wanted. Checking the brightness of the heated point, he placed it on the anvil where he hammered it with easy, efficient motions.

"It's been nice to make something like that," he said,

"after almost a full year of making pot hooks and hinges for tourist shops in Intercourse. Not that I'm complaining. Working here is when I feel closest to God." He was startled when those words came out of his mouth. Sensing any closeness with his Lord had been impossible for months.

She faced him. "How so? Because you're using the talents He gave you?"

"Partly." He fell back on the words he would have used before sorrow shadowed his days. "Also, it's because everything here from the coals on the forge to the iron to the stones on the floor beneath my feet was created by God. I'm using them to make something, too. Not that I can achieve the perfection of His creation, but I can praise Him for what He gave us for our use."

"I understand. I feel that way when I'm sewing, whether it's a garment or a quilt top or joining others in making a complete quilt."

Until he'd heard Clara talking with Leah on Sunday, he hadn't realized she was as knowledgeable about quilting as his sister-in-law was. But why should he? They hadn't spoken of much other than the Beachy twins.

As if he'd called their names, he saw the rear door of Amos's store open and the *kinder* rush out. They ran toward the forge, excited about the treats his brother had given them. When Clara moved to stand between the youngsters and the forge, he looked at Nettie Mae, who was smiling as she held up the candy bar she'd selected. How could he have failed to see she needed glasses?

He waved to them when Clara herded the *kinder* around the side of the building. Lowering his hand, he let his breath sift out past his taut lips. If anyone had asked him, he would have said—without a hint of doubt—he knew as much about the twins as their parents did.

But he'd been wrong.

That Nettie Mae was getting glasses was a pointed reminder he had to pay more attention to them. He should be relieved that he'd missed something as simple and innocuous as eyeglasses. He should be, but he wasn't.

What else didn't he know about Clara and the twins? Whatever he might learn, he'd better do it fast. The *kinder*'s family members could be arriving any day. The familiar pain rushed through him at the thought of never seeing them—or Clara—again. Maybe he'd be better off not knowing anything else, because when they left, knowing even a little bit more about them could make saying goodbye harder.

If possible.

Chapter Eight

Rain battered the windshield of his buggy as Isaiah reached the lane leading to the Beachys' house that evening. When lightning flashed followed by the slow, faraway rumble of thunder, a sure signal the storm was receding to the east, he hoped Clara had gotten home before it began. Though he'd thought she'd stop at the shop so he could see Nettie Mae's new glasses, she must have returned to get dinner started.

Or work in the garden, he corrected himself when he saw an abandoned basket of weeds beside the overgrown vegetable patch. The rain must have caught her and the youngsters unaware. Otherwise, Clara wouldn't have left the basket in the rain. After he finished his chores, he'd empty it on the compost pile and put the wooden slat basket in the mudroom to dry.

Bringing the buggy to a stop, he jumped out and went to unhitch Chip. The black horse didn't mind snow but hated rain.

"Let's go, boy," Isaiah said. "It's nice and dry in the stable." He glanced at the house. It would be pleasant in there as well, and he wondered what delicious meal Clara had prepared tonight.

He was no cook, but no matter how burned it was, he'd eaten every bite of the meals he'd made for himself when he lived alone in the small house he'd bought after his wedding. He'd counted himself blessed when he was asked to eat with his family or the Beachys. Either Esta or *Mamm* would have welcomed him every night, but often he'd worked late at his forge and didn't want to inconvenience anyone. *Mamm* was a great cook, and Esta had been less skilled, but much better than his fumbling attempts.

Clara, however, was a talented cook. Even something like her potato salad had an unexpected burst of flavor. She'd revealed that she added barbecue sauce and bacon to the usual ingredients.

Suddenly the door burst open. Andrew ran through the rain to fling his arms around Isaiah. "You're here!" the boy cried.

"*Ja*, I am, but are you supposed to be outside now?"

Instead of answering, the little boy asked, "Where have you been? *Aenti* Clara has had supper ready for a long, long time."

Isaiah flinched. What had Andrew called Clara? Pushing down a sudden rush of dismay, he said, "I'm sorry if you're hungry." He ruffled the *kind*'s wet hair. "Run inside and let her know I'll be in soon."

As the little boy raced away, Isaiah stood still. The rain fell around him and bounced off the brim of his hat. *Aenti* Clara? When had the *kinder* started calling her that? Had she asked them to?

He took the questions with him into the barn. They repeated in his mind in rhythm with the milker and followed him into the tank room where a diesel engine kept the milk cool until it could be pumped into the truck that collected it every day after he left for work.

One of the cows regarded him as she chewed on the hay in front of her stanchion. Her unblinking gaze seemed to ask him why he was upset. That the twins were comfortable with Clara should make him happy, so why was he questioning it? He hadn't been bothered when Amos had told him that the Beachy youngsters now called him *Onkel* Amos.

"They hope they can sweet-talk extra treats out of me," his brother had said with a laugh. "I don't know what you would have done if you hadn't found Clara to corral those youngsters. They've got so much energy."

Isaiah had agreed then, and he still agreed with his brother. So why did having the kids call Clara *aenti* set him on edge?

He dumped the last of the fresh milk through the filter and leaned one elbow on the stainless-steel milk tank. Looking across the small room, he knew he could keep on trying to ignore the truth, or he could start acknowledging it.

He envied the *kinder* who had let Clara into their lives. They didn't worry about what anyone else thought or how calling her *aenti* might complicate their lives. They accepted her kindnesses and her loving attempts to keep their days moving along without too much drama. She asked nothing of them other than to try to behave. If they didn't want to laugh, she wouldn't push them, though she was bothered by the situation. He needed to follow her example.

When Isaiah entered the house, Clara was busy at the stove. He greeted her and quelled his questions. There would be time later. After the twins were in bed. Tonight, somehow, he was going to make the effort to stay awake.

"Where are your glasses, Nettie Mae?" he asked as he sat at the table beside the little girl, who was pouting.

Her lower lip stuck out far beyond her top one, which she had sucked in close to her teeth. She must have been holding the glasses in her lap, because she tossed them on the table. Her siblings glanced at her, then away. They didn't want to be the target of her frustration.

"Those are cute, Nettie Mae," he said, as if he was oblivious to her mood.

"Ugly."

He was startled by her vehemence. Looking over her head to where Clara was placing sliced ham on the other end of the table, he said, "I think your glasses are cute, and I know you're cute, Nettie Mae. Why don't you put them on so I can see how cute you look with them?"

"No! Ugly." The little girl's nose wrinkled. "I no *grossmammi*."

"Not yet, you're not."

"*Grossmammi* wears eyeglasses. Not me."

Clara glanced at them with concern. She was worried he wasn't going to change the little girl's mind with logic. He needed to try something else.

"Can I see them?" he asked.

Nettie Mae slid them across the table to him. When he picked them up, he saw they were simple gold frames. The sides had been extended and curved so they went behind Nettie Mae's ears instead of on top of them. He guessed that would keep the glasses from flying off an active little girl's face.

Holding them in front of her, he said, "Please put them on so I can see them."

She knocked them out of his hand and onto the floor. "No!"

Everyone froze in the kitchen, including Isaiah. He wasn't quite sure what to do. He looked again at Clara. Did she have any idea?

Clara wished she knew what to say to stave off the angry words that could be coming next. Her *daed* would never allow her to defy him. The one time she'd been foolish enough to try, *Daed* had punished her severely. The pain from being lashed with his belt had worn off long before her fear of what would happen if she angered him again.

How would Isaiah react to Nettie Mae's blatant disrespect? She shuddered as she imagined him trying to bend the *kind*'s will as her *daed* had struggled to subdue hers. Nettie Mae's frustration wasn't aimed at him. She'd been uncooperative at the optician's, which was why Clara had brought the twins straight home.

Clara needed to act before the situation spiraled out of control, and little Nettie Mae paid the cost of her rebellion as Clara had. Picking up the gold-rimmed glasses, she blew on the lenses to dislodge any dust. She held them to her face as if she intended to try them on. Smiling, she offered them to the little girl.

Nettie Mae ignored her, turning her back and folding her arms across her chest.

Swallowing her gasp of shock, because to act so in her house would have meant a terrible punishment, Clara said, "Nettie Mae, Isaiah hasn't seen you wearing your glasses. Why don't you show him?"

She shook her head.

"*Mamm* wouldn't make her wear them!" Andrew said stoutly.

Bless him! He'd given Clara the opening she needed to defuse the situation. With a smile, she said, "Your *mamm* helped Nettie Mae pick them out and placed the order for them."

The little boy's eyes grew so big, white circled the bright blue in their center. "*Mamm* did?"

"Ja." Clara didn't add anything more. She waited to see how Andrew and Nettie Mae responded.

The two looked at each other, and she could see their certainty crumbling. Isaiah's shoulders relaxed. Had the despair lessened in his expression?

She squatted next to Nettie Mae's chair and placed the eyeglasses in the little girl's hand. She held her breath, hoping Nettie Mae wouldn't drop them again. When the *kind* hesitated, Clara gave her a bolstering smile.

Her eyes swimming in tears, the little girl set the glasses on her nose and settled the curved sides over her ears. A sob caught in the three-year-old's throat as she whispered, "I no *grossmammi.*"

"No, but you're a very pretty young lady," Isaiah said as he leaned toward her and rested his elbow on the table. "Don't you think so, kids?"

"But you say, *Onkel* Isaiah," argued Ammon, jumping into the conversation for the first time, "the prettiest thing is a smile."

"And when Nettie Mae smiles, you'll see it's true." He winked at the *kind*, who gave up her attempt to keep her smile off her face.

As her siblings began to smile, too, he turned to Clara. His gaze held hers, and his grin broadened. They were becoming an excellent team in dealing with the *kinder*.

The thought should have filled her with joy—and it did, but also sent a shiver of disquiet along her as she wondered how she was going to say goodbye to all of them.

"Whew!" Isaiah dropped heavily onto the sofa and leaned his head back, closing his eyes. "How can they have so much energy at the end of the day?"

Clara looked up from the letter she was folding and putting in an envelope. Like every other night, she and the *kinder* had spent time writing to their grandparents and *Aenti* Debra. It had become as much a bedtime ritual for them as brushing their teeth and saying their prayers. "Maybe they aren't tired because they don't have to chase themselves to make sure they stay out of trouble."

He smiled. "Not quite true. They do chase each other around, but in an effort to *find* mischief. I wonder what got them agitated tonight after Nettie Mae calmed down about her new glasses."

She shrugged. "They had an exciting day with the trip into town and the thunderstorm." She set the envelope with the other and the stamps on the table beside her. "I didn't realize how frightened they are of thunderstorms. All except Ammon, who seemed to take the loud crashes of thunder in his stride." Her eyes narrowed as she looked at where he was sprawled on the sofa. "What's wrong, Isaiah?"

"Nothing is wrong. Why do you ask?"

"You're here instead of heading to the *dawdi haus* as you've been doing every night this week, so I'm assuming you waited for the twins to go to bed to discuss something with me."

"Did anyone ever tell you that you've got too much insight into people?" He meant the question as a joke, but her face closed up as if she'd slammed a door between them.

"I learned as a *kind* to be aware of what other people were thinking so I'd know what they'd do." She ran her fingers over the envelopes. A nervous gesture, and he wondered why she was uneasy.

Maybe the best thing would be to end the conversation, but he needed one answer before he went into the *dawdi haus*, which had become a sanctuary where he didn't risk seeing Clara each time he turned around. "Can you tell me something? I'm curious how long the twins have been calling you *Aenti* Clara."

"Did one of them call me that?"

He couldn't doubt her surprise was genuine. "Andrew did tonight."

"I'll ask him not to, if it's bothering you. People might get the wrong idea." She chuckled. "*Onkel* Isaiah and *Aenti* Clara? You might as well put a target on your back for the matchmakers."

"That's not why I mentioned it."

"Oh?" Her wide eyes told him that he'd startled her again.

He leaned forward, resting his elbows on his knees. "It's clear to me that the *kinder* consider you part of their lives."

"But a temporary part."

"*Ja.*"

Coming to her feet, she clasped her hands in front of her. "Isaiah, what would you have me do? Treat the twins as if they're my job and nothing more?" She shook her head with a regretful smile. "I can't. *You* can't either. You were *wunderbaar* with Nettie Mae tonight, convincing her the glasses made her special."

"I think she's special, so why shouldn't she?"

"And that is what makes you special, Isaiah Stoltzfus."

"What? Helping a little girl realize she doesn't need to be a *grossmammi* to wear glasses?" He waved to dismiss her words. "Anyone would have done that."

"No." Her smile had vanished and regret remained. "Not everybody. I'm going to say something that you probably don't want to hear, but, Isaiah, your friends are right. You need to think of marrying because you're a very *gut daed*."

"That's not the reason to get married." He rolled his eyes. "Don't you dare mention this conversation to the Mast girls."

His attempt at teasing her fell flat because she remained serious. "You're a gift to these *kinder*. They know it, too. I'm beginning to wonder if that's why they're not as grief-stricken by their parents' deaths. They have you, and they know you'll take care of them as Melvin and Esta would have."

"But I'm not their *daed*."

"You are. At least temporarily."

Coming to his feet, he knew he needed to put an end to this conversation before it wandered from the twins to him and Clara. It would be such a small step, and one his heart was pushing him to take. No, he couldn't. Not when he knew how temporary this situation was. The *kinder*'s family should be arriving soon.

And what if he did listen to his heart? How could he be certain he wouldn't make a mess of everything with Clara as he had with Rose? He'd let his wife down by not being there when she needed him most. He could do the same with Clara, being so focused on his work he'd fail her when she depended on him to be there.

Look at how you've left her with all the work with the twins this past week, he reminded himself. *You didn't even have time to check the answering machine, and you drive by it twice a day.* He halted the thoughts. The gates would be on their way by week's end. In the meantime...

"Don't say anything to the twins about what they call you," he said.

"Are you sure?"

"*Ja*. If someone gets the wrong impression, that's their problem. I'd rather have the *kinder* comfortable with you."

She sat in the rocking chair again. "I agree."

"*Gut*. They are what's most important."

"Something else I can agree with."

He nodded. He doubted Clara did much without her heart being involved.

As she reached for the envelope and began writing on it, he asked, "Have you memorized their addresses already?"

"*Ja*." Looking up, she smiled, and his insides seemed to be jumping for joy. "The words in their street addresses are unusual. They stick in my mind."

He urged her to have a *gut* night's sleep and hurried toward the kitchen and the door to the *dawdi haus*. He wanted to get out of the main house before he said something stupid like saying how *she* stuck in his mind.

Chapter Nine

"Are you set for tomorrow?" asked Reuben as he reached for another slice of Wanda's delicious *snitz* pie.

Clara had been delighted with the invitation to the Stoltzfus farm for supper. She'd spent the day, while trying to do the household chores, watching Nettie Mae to see where the little girl stashed her glasses when she wasn't wearing them. Like in the center of the kitchen table or on the bathroom sink or in the middle of the living-room floor when she was showing off a picture she'd colored. So far, Clara had been able to keep them from getting broken. She'd been glad when Nettie Mae gave her the glasses to put in her pocket while they drove to Isaiah's family's farm a couple of miles along the twisting road.

She now joined in the celebration that Isaiah had finished the massive gates in time. The flatbed truck had come that morning.

The twins had been excited about seeing Isaiah's *mamm* whom they called *Grossmammi* Wanda. Or to be more accurate, Clara thought as she glanced out the window to where they were playing under the watchful eye of Leah's niece Mandy, to sample Wanda's desserts.

At the bishop's question, Isaiah sat straighter and frowned. "Oh, no! I forgot about tomorrow."

"What's tomorrow?" she asked as she picked up her sweating glass of ice tea.

"Saturday," Ezra said with a smile. He was Isaiah's next older brother, and he ran the dairy farm and oversaw its cheesemaking.

Leah slapped his arm. "Be polite."

"I'm always polite."

That brought a snort from Isaiah. "*Always* covers a lot of time and space, big brother." Without a pause, he turned to Reuben. "Do you think we can find someone else to go at this late date?"

Clara looked from one face to the other around the table. Isaiah was annoyed with himself for not planning for whatever was going to happen tomorrow, but nobody else seemed perturbed. She wanted to ask again what was going on and tried to be patient. The others would let her know if it was any of her business.

But Isaiah is my business, her thoughts insisted. *If something is upsetting him, it's bound to upset the kinder, and I need to be prepared.*

That was equivocating. She would be bothered whether or not Isaiah's problem with whatever was happening the next day disturbed the twins. After the tough times he'd faced the past month, he deserved a stress-free day or two.

Wanda came to her rescue by saying, "Clara, tomorrow is the annual youth trip to Hersheypark. Several months ago, Isaiah agreed to be a chaperone this year."

Without a pause, she asked, "Why don't you go with them, Clara?"

"Me?" She couldn't hide her astonishment.

"We'll watch the *kinder*." Wanda smiled. "Then you can do as you promised, Isaiah, and Clara can have a day off, too."

"But taking care of the twins is my job," she protested.

"Everyone should have a day off from their job once in a while." Reuben chuckled. "Even the *gut* Lord took a day off after creating the heavens and the earth."

"I can't argue with that."

"I told you that she has a lot of common sense," Isaiah said with a grin.

Wanda wagged a teasing finger at him. "You're saying that because you don't want to have to watch a bunch of teenagers by yourself."

"We won't be the only two chaperones, will we?" asked Clara.

Isaiah laughed, and she knew he was glad the *kinder* weren't there so he had to stifle his amusement. "No, there will be a couple more. Why are you uneasy about being with teenagers when you're outnumbered every day by *kinder*?"

"Because, as you said, I've got a lot of common sense. I know teenagers can think up mischief faster than preschoolers."

"That's *gut* to hear," Reuben said, "for this old man who'll be looking after little ones."

"You're going to help?" Clara asked, surprised. She'd assumed the twins would be cared for by Wanda and her daughter-in-law.

"Why not? It'll be *gut* practice for a man who hopes one of these days to be bouncing more *kins-kinder* on his knee." He sighed. "If one of my younger daughters would pick a young man and settle down..."

Wanda's secretive smile matched the twinkle in her eyes. "Let's talk later, Reuben. I might have a suggestion to help."

Isaiah grinned, and Clara could hear his thoughts as if he'd spoken aloud. He was pleased to have his *mamm* busy matchmaking for someone else. She lowered her gaze to the table, hoping to hide her delighted smile. It would be fun to spend time with Isaiah. Maybe they'd have time to talk about concerns she didn't want to discuss when the twins were around.

The past few nights, the *kinder* hadn't been as enthusiastic about writing to their grandparents and *aenti*. Their reluctance had begun after they asked her about leaving the only home they'd ever known to live with extended family. She'd told them the decision would be made by adults, and she'd seen the glances they'd exchanged. From then on, they'd come up with excuse after excuse not to include a drawing or colored picture with the letter. In fact, she'd written almost everything in the most recent letters.

She wanted Isaiah's opinion about how to handle the touchy situation. She wouldn't lie to the *kinder*, but she didn't want them to worry all the time.

Reuben cleared his throat, drawing her attention to the bishop. He dampened his lips before he asked, "Do the *kinder* speak of their parents?"

"Never," Clara replied.

"It's not right. Do you talk about Melvin and Esta with them?"

Isaiah shook his head. "Not very often, because we don't want to make them sad."

"My dear boy, nobody on God's green earth could make them sadder than they are." The bishop sighed.

"When I mention their parents," Clara said, "I let them take the lead in the conversation, but I urge them to talk."

"You do?" asked Isaiah.

She nodded. "Not that it matters. They change the subject. I get the feeling that sometimes one of them slips and breaks whatever agreement they've made not to speak of their parents. They immediately turn the conversation away from Melvin and Esta."

"Agreement?" Wanda frowned. "I don't like the sound of that. It's bad enough someone told them not to laugh. Did someone tell them to stay quiet about their parents?"

"Maybe." Isaiah scraped his palms on the edge of the table. "Who knows?"

"The *gut* Lord." His *mamm* patted his hands. "We need to let God guide the *kinder* and us."

Clara watched Isaiah as the others nodded. He copied the motion, but she could see he was having trouble agreeing. It confirmed what she'd suspected. Something stood between Isaiah and God. His friends' deaths? The tragic loss of his wife? A shadow hung over him, so dark and deep it was almost visible.

She didn't have the slightest idea how to ask him if she could help him. Or if she should. Knowing the truth would bring them closer, and she couldn't risk that.

The next day dawned warm and sunny. Not a cloud marred the perfect blue sky, and the humidity had been washed away by the night's rain. The *kinder* were picked up by Isaiah's younger brother Daniel, who planned to take them to the Stoltzfus farm. His betrothed, Hannah, her great-grandmother and her little sister Shelby, almost two years old, lived nearby in a house Daniel had built to showcase his talents as a carpenter.

"We're glad to have the twins join us," Daniel said with a broad smile that crinkled his eyes. "I was thinking of taking the *kinder* fishing."

"I hope you don't plan on catching anything." Isaiah clapped his brother on the shoulder.

"As long as I don't have to fish them out of the water, I'll consider it a successful day. Hannah and *Grossmammi* Ella will be joining us for a picnic along with *Mamm* and Reuben, so they'll have plenty of eyes on them, too. They'll have a great time with us."

"About telling them a joke—"

Daniel became serious. "*Mamm* warned me. Who would have told those cute kids not to laugh?"

"I'm hoping we can find out, so we can have him or her tell them it's okay to laugh now. If they smile, consider it a *gut* day for them."

"We'll have a *wunderbaar* day. Hope you will, too." He paused as his mouth twisted. "By the way, I know Katie Kay was supposed to go along on this trip…"

"Who's Katie Kay?" Clara asked.

"One of Reuben's daughters," Isaiah said at the same time Daniel replied, "Reuben's problem *kind*. She's run away."

"Reuben didn't say anything about that last night," she said.

"When he got home, he found out she was gone." Daniel sighed. "From what I was told, she's staying with an *Englisch* friend, and nobody knows when she'll come back home."

"Does Micah know?" Isaiah asked. "Clara, in case nobody's told you already, our brother Micah has had a gigantic crush on Katie Kay for a long time. Not that he's asked her if he could take her home. He doesn't talk to her because he's in awe of her."

"I'm not sure that's the case any longer," his brother said with a sigh. "Micah was pretty disgusted when he heard she'd argued with Reuben a couple of days ago. According to her sisters, she left in a huff last night, saying she wouldn't return until she was *gut* and ready."

Isaiah helped Clara get the *kinder* into his brother's buggy along with the plates of cookies and the ready-to-bake casserole she was sending along for their midday meal. Tomorrow, if Katie Kay hadn't come to her senses, he'd make sure to talk with Micah and Reuben. Especially Reuben, because in the past month, Isaiah had come to understand the depth of joy and pain a *kind* could bring to a *daed*'s life. Even a temporary *daed*'s.

He waited until Daniel's buggy had disappeared over a hill before he went into the house. Clara was checking the stove was off and no water dripped in the sink.

"Clara?"

She faced him.

"*Danki* for agreeing to come with me. Again I know it wasn't what you expected when you accepted the job of taking care of the twins."

"Why do you keep saying that?" Puzzlement filled her voice and expressive eyes.

"Saying what?"

"That this or that thing must not be what I expected when I took this job."

"Well, it couldn't have been."

She smiled. "Maybe not a trip to the amusement park, but I didn't come here with any assumptions. I've been surprised every day by big things and small."

"We didn't try to mislead you."

"Of course you didn't. Many of the surprises have been lovely ones like rediscovering how far a grasshopper can jump when trying to get away from youngsters intent on capturing it." Her smile faded. "Isaiah, you worry too much about things that can't be changed. Maybe shouldn't be changed."

He crossed the kitchen to close the distance between them. "Mostly I'm worried about one thing."

"What's that?" Her voice dropped to a husky whisper as she tilted her head to meet his gaze.

His heart halted in midbeat as he gazed into her brown eyes. They were delightfully close to his. A single lock of red hair had escaped her *kapp*, and he had to force his hand to remain by his side so he didn't reach out and twirl it around his finger. Its vibrant color was a tease as he envisioned loosening her hair and seeing it become a fiery fall down her back.

Then she took a step away. A single step, but the motion was enough to break the connection between them and let him escape from his imagination. Nothing had changed. He didn't trust himself to be there for another woman, so how could he ask this very special one to trust him?

"What are you worried about, Isaiah?" she asked, her words as shaky as his knees.

"Having you leave because you decide you don't want to put up with any more of the hassles you've faced since you've gotten here."

Startled, she repeated, "Leave?"

"If you go, Clara, I'm not sure what the twins and I would do. You've brought a serenity into the midst of the chaos exploding around us."

"What makes you think I'm going anywhere? I told you I'd be here, God willing, until the *kinder*'s family comes to collect them."

"I'm glad to hear that." He was. On many different levels in his heart, including ones he'd thought sealed forever.

"We need to get going, or we'll miss the bus," she said.

"Let's go." He closed the door behind him as he needed to shut out these yearnings. He cared too much about Clara to put her through the hard lessons of discovering how he could let her down.

An hour later, Isaiah was spending more time watching Clara than the five teenagers they were supposed to be chaperoning. The kids were looking around with interest, but she was gaping at the rides and the crowds inside the entrance. When she exclaimed over the bright colors and the delicious smells, the three boys and two girls with them giggled.

"You've never been to Hersheypark before, Clara?" Isaiah asked.

"Never. I know it's a tradition in your district for the teenagers to take this trip at least once every summer, but it wasn't in mine."

"Did you have any traditions?" He paused as the teens discussed whether they wanted to stop for funnel cakes or frozen yogurt first. The idea of either in the midmorning made his stomach protest.

"Of course! My favorite was when the youth groups had a picnic and went canoeing."

"Did you get dunked?"

"More than once, but everyone expected it, so we

brought extra clothes with us. Have you ever been out in a canoe?"

"A few times. The creeks around Paradise Springs get high enough in the spring to let us canoe, but by summer, they're trickles."

"I wonder if the twins would enjoy going out in a canoe. I could—"

He halted her by putting a finger to her lips. "Now, none of that." As the teens laughed, he lowered his voice while following them toward the first rides. "It's your day off, Clara. Remember what Reuben said. You don't have to think about the *kinder* today. They're in *gut* hands with my family. My *mamm* has raised nine of us, and Reuben has four daughters of his own as well as a son. Between them, they can handle two sets of mischievous twins."

"I know." She stopped again as the teens decided on hot dogs. When a boy asked if she wanted one, Isaiah was surprised when she nodded and ordered one with ketchup and relish. "But it's difficult *not* to think about them."

He grinned and said as she had, "I know. They're a part of my life." His smile faded. "I don't like to think of a time when they won't be."

"Their *aenti* lives in California, right?"

"When she's not on mission work." He sighed, wishing the conversation hadn't taken this turn. He'd looked forward to having a day with Clara and getting to know her better. "And the twins' grandparents live in Pinecraft, Florida. They belong to a Mennonite church there. When Esta fell in love with Melvin, she accepted our way of life and was baptized before they married."

"Having someone, even a conservative Mennonite, join our church doesn't happen often."

"As you may have noticed, each of the twins has a

stubborn streak a mile wide. They got that from Esta."
His smile returned when the boys brought over one hot
dog for Clara and two for him. "And a little bit more
from Melvin."

"And a little bit from you, too."

"Bad habits—as well as *gut* ones—tend to rub off
on people."

The teenagers led them from ride to ride, each one
more outrageous than the one before it. They laughed
as they rode the inanimate horses of the carousel and
squealed with excitement on the more adventurous rides.
It was a toss-up who enjoyed it more: the teenagers or
the chaperones.

The day passed quickly, and too soon one of the teenagers with a cell phone told them that they had one hour
before they had to leave. That set off a debate among the
boys about which rides they should go on. Isaiah stayed
out of the discussion while Clara and the girls went to
get sodas for everyone.

At the call of his name, he took a deep breath. He'd
seen Orpha Mast get on and off the bus ahead of him and
Clara. Someone on the bus must have mentioned he was
chaperone. Most likely Larry Nissley, one of the biggest
gossips in Paradise Springs, who'd stepped off the bus
right after Orpha.

Orpha, wearing a bright cranberry dress, smiled. "Are
you having a fun day, Isaiah?"

"I can't imagine anyone not having fun at Hersheypark."
He resisted glancing toward the restaurant where Clara
had gone with the girls. When he saw Larry hanging by
its door, he had to fight not to frown. Was Larry watching them? Or just Orpha? "You'd have to try hard in order
not to have fun."

"True." She stepped closer, seeming oblivious to the looks the boys—and Larry—shot in their direction. "But it's seldom I get to do anything fun. You don't know how it is in our house."

"I know your family is very close."

Her eyes narrowed as she frowned. "I thought you were insightful. At least, that's what Rose told me. She said you'd guessed the truth of why she married you."

"She married him," said Clara as she came to stand next to them, "because she loved him. That's what everyone has told me."

"*Everyone* doesn't know the truth." Orpha tapped the center of her chest. "I do. She married you, Isaiah, because *Daed* has ordered us to marry before our twenty-first birthday. You were available, so she married you."

Clara stiffened, but her face remained serene as she looked at Orpha as if the other woman were as young as the twins. Her voice remained calm when she said, "That's enough of your vitriol, Orpha. I'm sorry if your *daed* insists you marry by a certain date. Many parents do, but you don't see the rest of us venting our annoyance." Not letting the other woman answer, she added, "Don't listen to her, Isaiah. She's trying to hurt you. You don't have to believe her—"

"No, you don't have to believe me," Orpha snapped, "but you'll believe Leah, ain't so? Rose said she told Leah the truth one day. Ask Leah!"

"What's in the past is in the past." Isaiah appreciated Clara coming to his defense, but it was unnecessary. "Nothing we say or do can change what's happened." He looked from one teenager to the next and saw none of them were surprised by Orpha's outburst. They knew her too well. "We've got time for one more ride. What'll it be?"

He walked away with their group, letting the teens take the lead. Though he kept a handbreadth between him and Clara, he was as aware of her vexation as if it were his.

"Don't dwell on Orpha's words," he said.

"How can you let her say such hateful things to you?" Clara asked, her tone taut.

"How could I stop her?"

She sputtered for a moment, then said, "You're right."

"Clara, no matter what reason Rose had for marrying me, she came to love me. More than I deserved, to be honest."

"Why do you say that?"

He hesitated on his answer, not wanting to darken the day with a litany of his mistakes. But wasn't saying nothing almost as bad as lying?

When one of the boys turned and called that they wanted to ride the Kissing Tower, a round observation tower decorated on the outside by gigantic candy Kisses, Isaiah was grateful he didn't have to answer Clara's question. The five teenagers bounced around them like a mob of kangaroos.

They waited in line at the tall tower. When it was their turn, he motioned for Clara to precede him onto the ride. Entering the circular cabin that moved up and down a cylinder as wide as a silo and twice as tall, she waited for him before she moved toward the teens who were looking out the windows, trying to determine which one would give them the best view.

Clara gazed out, too, as the ride started to rise and then begin to turn to offer vistas of the park and the countryside around it, but Isaiah couldn't take his eyes off her. She was a fascinating collection of contrasts. She showed many of her emotions, but hid others so deeply he couldn't guess what they might be. She was loving with the *kinder*, and, at the same time, she taught them to do what was right. She spent at least an hour each night writing to the youngsters' family, but seldom spoke of hers.

And the one aspect of her that puzzled him most was how she could be alluring without being flirtatious. In fact, it was the opposite. She treated him as a partner in caring for the *kinder*, and she'd agreed to let the matchmakers have their fun without it meaning anything. The few times his resolve had slipped and he'd considered drawing her to him, she'd found a way to edge away.

He grimaced when he thought of how different the day would have gone if Orpha had been with him instead of Clara. She would have hung on his every word and on his arm whenever she could manage it. Rather than enjoying the rides, she would have seen them as an opportunity to nestle up to him.

He would have liked Clara to cuddle close on one of the rides. She'd slid across the seat and bumped into him on the Tilt-A-Whirl, but pushed herself to her side as she laughed. He should have gathered her to him while they enjoyed the ride together.

Stop it! he warned himself. That he liked spending time with Clara was no reason to think of her as anyone other than the woman hired to help him take care of the Beachy twins. Within a few weeks, she'd be back at her family's farm and the *kinder* gone. He'd again be concentrating on work at the blacksmith shop and as a minister. Hadn't he learned how painful it was to imagine a future that could be snatched away?

His gaze went again to Clara. It would hurt her, too, to be separated from the twins. Would she miss him, as well?

The Kissing Tower reached its apex over two hundred feet from the ground, and he saw a few of the *Englisch* riders kissing. Though he considered it an excellent idea, he stood beside Clara and pretended he didn't see the public displays around them.

"Isn't it beautiful?" she asked, as her fingers squeezed his before releasing his hand.

"Beautiful," he agreed, his gaze focused on her.

"I've had a great time today, Isaiah."

"I'm glad I got to spend your first day at Hersheypark with you."

"I am, too."

He wanted to grab her hand and hold on to it, but he was here to keep an eye on the teenagers, not expect them to chaperone him and Clara. Yet, after spending these *wunderbaar* hours with her at the theme park, he was unsure how he'd recover from her departure. In some ways, Clara's leave-taking would be harder to endure than Rose's. He'd loved Rose. He'd married her and dreamed of them starting a family. He'd known from the beginning that Clara was in Paradise Springs a short time. So why would her leaving shred his scarred soul?

Clarity struck him as the circular ride neared its base again. Rose hadn't chosen to leave. Clara would. Once the twins were settled with their extended family, she would pack her buggy and drive away.

And he'd be alone again.

More alone than after Rose's death, because nobody would know he was enduring another loss. He wouldn't have Melvin, who had stood by him in his darkest hours when living had seemed like too great a burden.

Clara didn't notice his silence on the trip home. She was kept too busy chatting with the girls they'd spent time with at the park. Then they picked up the *kinder* from the farm, and the twins spent every minute of the ride home talking about playing with Mandy and Shelby and the fish they hadn't caught.

As soon as the buggy stopped, Clara said, "Let's write a letter to your *grossdawdi* and *grossmammi* after dinner, and I'll tell them about my day at the same time I'm telling you. And you can tell me about your day so we can put it in the letter, too. How does that sound?"

The *kinder* all nodded at the same time.

Isaiah asked, "Would you boys like to help me get the grill going? We'll have hamburgers."

"Ja!" shouted Andrew.

Ammon echoed him a moment later as both boys ran to the storage barn where the grill was kept.

"Leave the charcoal alone!" Isaiah called after them. "I'll get it!" Lowering his voice, he said, "The last time they *helped*, their clothes needed to be washed twice to get the grit out of them."

She smiled as she held her hands out to the girls. Each took one, and he watched them walk into the house. The girls leaned their heads against her, and she put an arm around each *kind*'s shoulders. Anyone driving by who didn't know better would think the three were the perfect image of a *mamm* and her *kinder*.

How easy it'd been to say the past was in the past. It was much more complicated to think of the future. Anything was possible in the days and weeks and months and years ahead of them.

He walked away before the sight tempted him toward thoughts he must not have.

Yet he did. Far too often.

Chapter Ten

Three days later, Clara was astonished to see Isaiah waiting in the kitchen when she came downstairs to start breakfast. Usually, at this hour just before dawn, he'd be out to the barn doing chores. She was about to ask him if everything was okay when the stern expression on his face told her it wasn't.

"There's been a death at the Gingerich house. Henry Gingerich," he said without a preamble. "A heart attack in his sleep. I need to get over there to help the family."

"I'm sorry to hear that. Do you want me to pack food for you to take with you?"

He shook his head. "No. There will be plenty there. You know how plain folks make sure the grieving family has more to eat than they need." His eyes shifted toward the freezer compartment on the refrigerator. He swallowed so hard she could see the motion.

Though the last of the food brought for Melvin and Esta's funeral had been used up, she guessed he couldn't get the picture of the stuffed freezer out of his mind. It was a lingering reminder of his loss.

"Is there anything else I can do?" she asked.

"Will you explain to the kids that I may not be able to get to their picnic at school?" He raked his hand through his pale hair, leaving it spiked across the top of his head.

She resisted the temptation to smooth those strands. "Don't worry. I'll make sure the boys see everything at school."

"I promised Andrew and Ammon I would attend with them."

"I know."

The older twins had been excited last night about visiting the school they'd attend in the fall. Neva Fry had taken over the school when Isaiah's younger sister, Esther, married, and, as the new teacher, Neva had decided to ask next year's first-time students to attend school for a fun day so the building and scholars would be familiar to them on their first day. In addition, she asked the parents to join in a frolic of cleaning the school building and yard.

With the gates done, Isaiah had looked forward to spending time with the twins at the school gathering. He'd volunteered to help paint the small outhouses used by the scholars. The buckets of white paint were already in the family buggy. Neither Isaiah nor Clara had mentioned that the twins might not be in Paradise Springs in the fall. Until they knew for sure who was going to take them and where, there was no reason to disrupt the *kinder* further.

"The twins will understand," she said, though she wasn't sure.

"If you tell them I've gone to oversee plans for a funeral." His face lost what little color it'd had. "But I don't want them to know that. Not on such a special day."

She put her hand on his arm. "Go and be with the Gingerich family. They need you more than the *kinder* do."

"I'm not sure about that."

"I am. Let me do what you hired me to do."

He put his hand over hers, and she found herself sinking into the depths of his blue-gray eyes. She wished she knew how to answer the questions she saw within them. If she tried, everything would change between them. She couldn't risk her heart again. The cracks in it were welded together by the heat of the tears she'd cried.

"I hate dumping this on you," he said in a whisper.

"Don't you think I know? I'll try to keep them from hearing about Henry for as long as I can."

He nodded. "The boys have looked forward to this day."

"Nettie Mae and Nancy, too."

"I don't want it ruined for them."

"It won't be. Nobody is going to want to upset the scholars today." She hesitated, then asked, "Do you think you'll be able to get there later?"

"I don't know at this point."

There was so much regret in his voice her hand rose and curved along his smoothly shaven cheek above his wispy beard. "I'm sorry *you* have to miss today, Isaiah. After your hard work on those gates, you were due time to have fun with the twins."

He put his fingers over hers and gave her a sad smile. "We'll have to find another way to enjoy a fun day with them." Drawing her hand away from his face, he gave it a squeeze before he walked to the door. "I'll definitely be home in time for milking tonight."

She nodded, holding her lower lip between her teeth.

If she spoke, she wasn't sure she could silence the words she wanted to say. Words to tell him again how sorry she was he couldn't join them for the day as well as words to let him know how important he was becoming to her. She couldn't say *that*! It would mean putting her heart on the line again, and she wouldn't, especially when her time with him and the *kinder* was going to end too soon.

"We're going to school! We're going to school!" Andrew had turned the words into a song, which he sang at the top of his lungs, as he led the way out of the house.

When the other youngsters joined in, Clara made a big show of raising her hands as if to put them over her ears. Instead, she joined in, shocking the kids. They grinned, but she didn't hear the laughter she'd hoped for. She had to believe it would come one day.

She skipped with them to the buggy and, after cautioning them not to tip over the plates on the seats, motioned for them to climb in. She handed one plate to each *kind*.

"*Onkel* Isaiah isn't coming?" asked Andrew as he settled his covered plate on his lap, holding it with both hands.

She shook her head as she gave Nettie Mae a box containing the flatware they'd use. "He's meeting with Reuben today." It wasn't a lie, because the bishop would be at Henry Gingerich's house, too.

"But he said he was coming." Andrew stuck out his lower lip. "He told me last night he'd let me help paint."

"The paint is in the back of the buggy, and I'm sure, if you ask, the men painting the outhouses will let you help."

Nancy interjected, "*Onkel* Isaiah gonna push me on the swings till I kick the clouds."

"The next time you see him, ask him to take you there and give you a ride on the swings." To ward off more questions, she said, "Don't forget. Your *onkel* Isaiah knows the school well. He went there when he was a boy."

The *kinder* looked at her with astonishment. She couldn't tell if they were more surprised about Isaiah attending the same school they would or the fact he'd once been as young as they were.

Driving the buggy to the end of the farm lane, Clara asked, "Whose turn is it to get the mail today?"

"Mine!" Nancy jumped down from the buggy and ran to the metal mailbox where the letters spelling the family's last name were hardly visible. The door on the front had rusted away. Standing on tiptoe, she reached in. "A letter!" She waved it in the air as she rushed to the buggy. "For me?"

Clara took the envelope and turned it over to read the return address. "It's from your *aenti* Debra. Shall we read it now or after we go to school?"

"Now!" Nancy, Nettie Mae and Andrew shouted at the same time. Ammon chimed in a moment later...as he often did.

Too often did, Clara realized. He didn't wait for Andrew to speak for the twins, but let the younger girls also answer first. She'd thought he was shy but didn't believe that any longer. Once he joined in, he could be louder than the other three put together. Why was he the last one to answer any question she asked? And not only her questions, but everyone's.

She opened the thin envelope and pulled out a single piece of lined paper. The words were in such tiny handwriting she was tempted to borrow Nettie Mae's glasses.

"What does she say?" asked Andrew.

"Let's see," she said to buy herself time. Much of what Debra Wittmer had written wasn't suitable for the *kinder*. They didn't need to know about the number of deaths from recent earthquakes and the deprivations being prevented by the Mennonite mission. She began to read aloud the sections that were appropriate for the twins, the parts where Debra described the soaring landscapes and the nice people she'd met and worked with.

"Does she have a llama?" asked Nettie Mae when Clara paused to take a breath.

Pretending to check, Clara said, "She says the local people do and that the llamas carry goods for them when they shop in the village."

"I like llamas," the little girl said with a smile. "Can we ask *Aenti* Debra to bring one home?"

"Llamas live in herds like cows do. A llama by itself would be very lonely."

"But we'd love it!"

"I know, but a llama wants to be with other llamas, and you wouldn't want it to be lonely, would you?" Going back to "reading" the letter, Clara finished with, "It's signed with your *aenti* Debra's name."

"Right there," Ammon said, leaning over the seat to point at the letters. "*D-e-b-r-a*. That spells Debra."

"It does." She smiled at him. "Are you sure you haven't already been going to school? You know your ABC's, ain't so?"

"*Mamm* helped me," he whispered before he sat on the back bench.

Andrew sniffed and rubbed his hand against his nose as he dropped next to his brother.

"You learned very well," Clara said, not wanting to let silence settle on the buggy. Her heart ached for the *kinder*.

If she'd had any doubt, the broken expressions on their young faces would have confirmed—for once and for all—that the twins were suffused with grief. She wanted to gather them into her arms and hold them until they let down the walls that must take an untold amount of will to keep in place.

Who were you who told them not to laugh and not to grieve? Why did you deny them the very tools that could allow them to heal?

By the time she reached the schoolhouse, Clara had gotten her unsteady emotions under control. She helped the *kinder* carry the food and supplies to the porch. They put the plates next to what others brought. She'd thought the twins would rush off to join the other kids, but they clung close to her. Another sign of how ragged their feelings were.

A young woman with a warm smile approached them. "I'm Neva Fry, the teacher here. I saw you at the most recent church Sunday, Clara."

"Andrew and Ammon will be joining you in the fall." *If their family doesn't move them away from Paradise Springs*, she added silently as she put one hand on each boy and gave them a gentle shove forward.

Neva asked, "Would you like to see inside the school? *Komm*. I'll show you."

The boys' enthusiasm returned, though they didn't budge far from Clara, as the teacher pointed out where they'd be sitting in the front row with the other youngest scholars. She urged them to sit at the desks and page through the books they'd be using. Andrew seemed more interested in the desk itself, but Ammon ran his finger along the words in the primer and mouthed each letter to himself.

It was the last time either of them sat all morning. While Clara helped the scholars' *mamms* give the classroom a *gut* cleaning, including every hidden space in the desks, the youngsters played outside under the supervision of Neva's assistant teacher.

Clara was pleased to discover Leah among the other volunteers. They worked together washing the windows with vinegar and water until the glass sparkled.

When it was time for their picnic meal, adults had arranged the food, making sure there were serving utensils with each dish. Neva called to her scholars who were waiting to eat. A girl and boy came over and smiled at her when she asked if they'd share their blankets, spread on the grass, with the older twins. They nodded and offered their hands to Andrew and Ammon.

Andrew grabbed the boy's hand, leaving the girl to his brother. Ammon hesitated before grasping the girl's hand, but both boys were grinning as the older *kinder* chatted with them about school.

"He's too young to think girls have cooties," Neva said, as she smiled at Clara. "Most of the girls and boys play with each other until they're around ten or eleven years old."

Clara returned the smile to be polite, but her gaze followed the twins. Again and again, Ammon glanced at his brother before acting. It was as if he sought a clue to what he should do next. Ammon followed his brother's lead. There must be a reason why the little boy was dependent on his twin.

Helping the little girls select what food they wanted from the vast variety on the porch, Clara led them to where Leah was sitting beside her niece. Mandy began talking with the twins who hung on every word. Several times, Clara had to remind them to eat.

"They're adorable," Leah said. "It seems like such a short time ago Mandy was no older than they are. Enjoy them, Clara."

"I do."

"Do you know when their grandparents are returning?"

"I haven't heard from them, but the missionary board said it'd be at least another week or two before they could get home. At the earliest."

"Isaiah is going to miss the *kinder* if they leave."

"I know. We all will."

Leah put her fork on her plate and set both beside her on the grass. "I worry about Isaiah. To lose them on top of losing their parents so soon after Rose died... It would break a weaker man."

Clara jumped in to ask before she could stop herself, "Did Rose tell you that she married him because her parents insisted?"

"Who told you that?" She held up her hands. "No, I know who did, and I'm sure it was when Isaiah could hear, too. I don't know how Orpha thinks she can persuade Isaiah to marry her when she acts spiteful."

"Rose didn't tell you that her parents insisted she get married?"

"She told me, but she also said she married Isaiah because she loved him. I wasn't in Paradise Springs when they courted. I was here during the short time they were married, however. I never doubted she loved him. It's true she was horrified when the lot fell on him, because she didn't believe she would make a *gut* minister's wife. She tried her best before she died."

"Will you tell Isaiah that? He's filled with a terrible guilt about his marriage."

Leah put her hands on Clara's arms. "I've told him that Rose loved him. Over and over. Help him, Clara. After seeing him with you, I think you may be the only one who can."

Clara rolled her eyes. "Please. No matchmaking."

"I'm not talking about you marrying him. I'm talking about you *helping* him lay his past to rest along with whatever guilt he's carrying around with him."

"I want to, but I don't know how."

"I think you do." Leah's smile softened. "I think your heart does. All you need to do is listen to it."

Was it that simple? Even if it was, doing so meant giving her heart free rein. It already yearned to lead her to Isaiah. Yet, how could she *not* help him?

Her thoughts spun around in her head until she heard Neva call, "Who wants to play softball? Andrew? Ammon? Do you want to play?"

Andrew's head whipped around the moment the teacher spoke his name, but Ammon continued to watch the other *kinder* rushing to the spot where teams could be chosen. Jumping to his feet, Andrew gave his brother's arm a gentle slap. Ammon looked at him. When Andrew motioned for his twin to follow him, he did.

Clara stared after them as the truth battered her. Ammon couldn't hear everything said by her or anyone else. He was taking his signals from his siblings, going along and trusting them that they would clue him in on what was happening.

Had Isaiah noticed? She had to tell him about her suspicions as soon as possible.

As he stopped his buggy behind others parked in front of the schoolhouse, Isaiah heard the scholars cheering. Their excitement was what he needed to lift his heart. Preparations for a funeral were never easy, even when the person who'd died was old and in pain.

He'd known Henry Gingerich all of his life. The elderly farmer had been part of the lives of almost everyone in the district because he always helped his neighbors and family. By the next day, vans would be arriving at the Gingerich house, bringing family members who lived too far away to come by buggy.

Tomorrow he'd take each twin aside and tell them what had happened. He doubted they'd know who Henry Gingerich was, though they'd seen him almost every church Sunday of their lives.

As he stepped out of the buggy, a pair of small blurs rushed toward him.

"*Onkel* Isaiah!" shouted Nancy.

Nettie Mae threw her arms around him as if she hadn't seen him in weeks rather than a few hours.

He stopped and gave the little girls each a hug. Tapping Nettie Mae's nose beyond her glasses, he grinned. "Have you been coloring?"

"*Ja! Komm* and see. My dog! Want one."

"A dog?"

"Like Shelby's."

Having no idea what the little girl was talking about, he knew he'd have to ask Daniel what sort of dog—and if it was real or stuffed—the toddler had.

"You here!" Nancy cried. "Me glad!"

"*Ja*, me too." He looked past her. Clara was walking toward them. What would she do if he held out his arms to her as he had to the *kinder*? It was sweet to imagine her stepping into them, because her head was at the perfect height to lean against his shoulder.

"Go and get a ladle of cold water for your *onkel* Isaiah," Clara said. As soon as the girls had sped away, she turned to him. "You look exhausted."

"I feel like I've been carrying an elephant around."

"How's the family doing?"

"There's sadness, but knowing he went in his sleep is a blessing for the whole family. I—" He was struck from behind twice, hitting him hard enough to knock the breath out of him. Expecting the girls, he was surprised to see the boys throwing their short arms around him.

"You're here! You're here!" Andrew cried.

Beside him, Ammon nodded, his eyes glistening with tears.

Tears? Why would the little boy cry at the sight of a man he called his *onkel*?

As if he'd asked that question aloud, Clara said, "They've been anxious that you wouldn't come…" She pressed her fingers to her lips as her eyes widened.

At the motion, comprehension burst through him as it must have through her. He realized what the *kinder* meant. They hadn't been concerned he wouldn't come to the picnic. They were concerned he wouldn't come home at all.

As their parents hadn't.

With stark dismay, he recalled how one often clung to him when he left for work. They were as excited when he arrived at day's end as if he'd been gone for days instead of hours.

He couldn't promise he'd always make his way home

to them. Life changed without warning, as they knew too well.

Soon, the *kinder* would be with their real family. How long would it take for them to forget him? He knew how long it would take him to forget them. Forever and a day. They were as much a part of him as his next breath. And within a couple of weeks, they'd be gone. Just as Melvin and Esta were.

The grief striking him was like a fist to the gut. He turned away so none of them could see his face.

Andrew's name was called, and he looked over to where the other *kinder* were waiting for him to take his place as the batter. When Isaiah motioned for him to go and play, both boys ran to the game.

"How do we get through to them that they'll never be alone?" asked Isaiah with a sigh.

"I don't know," Clara said, "but I think it's important they learn to be happy again."

He clasped his hands behind him so he wouldn't reach out to take hers. "I keep trying to remind myself that, but then I see the emptiness of my life without them, and my heart breaks again."

"Put them in God's hands, Isaiah, and trust He'll watch over them." She gave a nervous half laugh. "Sorry. I shouldn't be telling a minister to have faith."

"Why not? A minister is a man like any other. Having doubts or needing to reexamine one's faith is part of being human."

"You don't believe…?"

"*Ja*, I believe. That won't change."

"But?"

He shrugged. "Sometimes I'm not as close to God as I'd like to be."

"Are you angry with Him?"

He was about to give her a quick answer, but then he paused. Anger? Was that what he felt? Or was it disappointment or betrayal? He wouldn't be less than honest with her. "I don't know."

"You need to figure it out, or you'll never be happy again either."

"You're not telling me anything I haven't thought about myself. What I need is a solution."

"The answer is the same for you as for the twins. You must be willing to speak of your loss and mourn before you can accept it."

"I talk about Rose a lot."

"You talk about her death, but you seldom say anything about her life. Since I got here, I've learned about how Leah was gone from Paradise Springs for ten years before she returned with her niece. I found out Rebekah's first husband was best friends with your brother Joshua before his death. I know from personal experience your *mamm* makes the best *snitz* pie in the county."

"Everyone knows that."

"The point is, Isaiah, I know a lot about your family because they talk about each other in loving ways, but nobody talks about Rose. Or if they do, they stop when you come near."

"I didn't realize that."

"They love you. They don't want to add to your grief." She put a consoling hand on his arm. "I would be willing to listen if you need an ear."

"Danki." What else could he say? *Holding you will help me more than you listening to me? That when I look into your eyes, I can believe—if only for a second—*

I'm not a lousy human being who failed the person who trusted me most?

When she started to say something else, he didn't give her time. He walked toward the ball game where he could submerge his guilt and sorrow behind a practiced smile once more.

Chapter Eleven

For the first time, the evening seemed to drag for Clara. It shouldn't have, because the *kinder* had had an exciting day. The boys shared every detail of visiting the school with Isaiah. When they paused to take a breath, the girls jumped in with their impressions of the school, Neva, the scholars and everything else they'd seen. Each of the *kinder* had a different favorite memory. Andrew liked playing ball. Nettie Mae was delighted with the artwork hanging on the school's walls, and Nancy asked when they could return to play on the swings and have Isaiah swing her high again. Ammon didn't say much until Isaiah asked him, point-blank, what he'd liked best. He considered for a moment and then announced he'd liked the food.

Clara tried not to show her impatience as she prepared a quick supper of ham sandwiches while Isaiah did the barn chores. She was tempted to skip one night of writing a letter with the *kinder*, but they'd insisted. They wanted to tell *Aenti* Debra about their visit to the school.

"Let her know we're big enough to go to school in

the fall," Andrew said at least a dozen times. "Me and Ammon."

"I will," she replied each time, but made the letter shorter than usual. She was glad when the twins didn't seem to notice, and she folded the page and put it in its envelope, sealing it.

After persuading the twins to go to sleep after an extra story was read in the hope of calming them, Clara came downstairs. Isaiah had left the twins' bedroom right after their prayers, and she saw the door to the *dawdi haus* was closed.

She paused long enough to check the letter from Debra was in her pocket before she went to the connecting door. She rapped and called, "Isaiah?" When she didn't get an answer, she knocked again. "Isaiah, may I speak with you about the *kinder*?"

She heard the lock slide on the other side. Was he using it for propriety's sake or to shut the rest of them out? No, that made no sense because she'd seen the faint shadows of loneliness in his eyes when he spoke of the twins going with their family.

"What is it, Clara?" he asked.

At his abrupt tone, she considered waiting until the morning. No, she couldn't. Too much was at stake.

"May I come in and speak to you about a couple of things with the twins?" she asked.

"Ja." He pushed the door open wider, then backed away so she could enter.

As she went in, he vanished into the bedroom. Not knowing what else to do, she pulled out a chair at the table in the center of the main room. She folded her hands on the table and waited.

Isaiah was wiping his hands on a towel as he came out

of the bedroom. Without a word, she held out the letter from Debra. He took it and opened the envelope. He read the page before he folded it again and handed it to her.

"She didn't ask anything about the *kinder*," he said as he sat facing Clara. "Nothing about her coming for them."

"I noticed that, too, but the date on the letter is almost three weeks ago. She probably hadn't received a letter from the twins when she wrote this one."

"But you'd have thought she'd ask about future arrangements for them."

"I've been wondering if she's waiting to hear from their grandparents first."

He gave her a dim smile. "You may be right, Clara. The two sides of the family have to agree. I'm sure more letters are on their way."

"I hope so." She gripped the edge of the table as she went on to the real reason she'd intruded on his privacy. "We need to talk about Ammon. I think there's something wrong."

"Is he sick?"

"No. *Ja.*"

"Which is it?"

"I don't know." She began to relate what had happened that afternoon.

His face became grim as he listened, and, though she could see questions in his eyes, he waited until she was finished before he asked, "And you think he's having trouble hearing?"

"*Ja.* Do you know if he's had a lot of ear infections or allergies? Some kids when I was growing up had one or the other, and sometimes they had trouble hearing when their ears were stopped up."

"With four young kids, it seems like one or another is sick all winter. I can't remember anything specific."

"Do you know if Esta kept any medical records for them?"

"I know she had their immunization records, but I don't know about anything else. If she did keep a record, it would be in the top drawer of the dresser in their bedroom."

"Oh." She had closed the bedroom door the morning after her arrival, and it hadn't been opened since... as far as she knew. Maybe Isaiah had gone inside, but she hadn't, and none of the *kinder* had either. "I'll go and check."

"No, I will." He squared his shoulders. "Wait here. It won't take long."

She watched him leave. It would be heart-wrenching for him to enter the room that had been the private retreat of his best friend and his wife. She folded her hands in front of her and bent her head until her forehead was against her clasped thumbs. Her wordless request was for God to be with Isaiah during his search. She didn't raise her head or stop repeating the request until she heard his footsteps in the kitchen.

Making sure that her *kapp* was in place and she revealed no sign of her despair, she gave him a slight smile when he returned to the *dawdi haus*. She didn't say anything about the lines of tension cutting into his face as if he'd aged years while he was gone.

"This was all I could find." As he sat at the table again, he held out four small bright orange booklets that were folded in the center. "Their shot records. You look at these two." He tossed them in front of her. "I'll go through the other two, and we'll see which one is Ammon's. Maybe

Esta wrote something in there to help us understand why he seems to be having trouble hearing."

The first booklet she opened was Nettie Mae's, and Clara's hopes rose when she saw a note about the little girl needing to have her eyes checked. Closing it, she opened the other. It belonged to Andrew and contained only the dates of his immunizations.

Looking at Isaiah, she said, "You must have Ammon's."

"I do, but there's nothing in it to help." He handed it to her, and she saw it was identical to Andrew's. A shot record. Nothing else.

Showing him the words in Nettie Mae's, she asked, "Do you think Esta hadn't realized Ammon might be having trouble hearing?"

"*I* hadn't noticed until you said something."

She hesitated, then said, "I'd like him to see a *doktor*. If there's a problem, it's something we need to know before he starts school in the fall."

"I agree."

She breathed a silent sigh of relief. *"Gut."*

His brows lowered. "Did you think I would say no to taking Ammon to have his hearing tested?"

"No."

"At least you sound certain."

"I am." She looked at the orange booklets. "I wish I could be sure we're doing the right thing."

"How can it be the wrong thing? If his hearing is okay, we'll work with Dr. Montgomery to discover what might be the problem."

"Let's take it one step at a time."

He stroked her fingers as he said, "A *gut* idea."

As she smiled, she wondered if he was talking about the boy or if the subject had shifted to the two of them.

Once Ammon had seen Dr. Montgomery at the medical clinic in Paradise Springs, an appointment with an audiologist was set up for three days later. It was in Lititz, too far away to go by buggy. Clara called Gerry, the *Englisch* van driver Wanda suggested.

The twins enjoyed the short ride in the van to the Stoltzfus farm. Andrew was fascinated by the elderly driver who was as much a baseball fan as the boy was. Soon Gerry and Andrew were chatting like old friends about the Philadelphia team and Andrew's favorite, the Pittsburgh Pirates.

At the familiar white farmhouse, Wanda and Leah along with Mandy were waiting for the twins. Ammon looked uncertain when the other *kinder* got out and then Isaiah climbed in the van, closing the door.

Clara had explained to the boy, as Dr. Montgomery had, why he was going for the testing and that there wouldn't be any needles or bad-tasting medicine involved. Even so, the little boy sat stiffly during the half-hour drive northwest to Lititz.

Beyond the center of the pretty village, Gerry flipped on his turn signal and pulled into a long, low shopping plaza. For a moment, Isaiah thought the *Englischer* had made a wrong turn; then he saw the name of the audiology company on one of the storefronts. When Isaiah noted a nearby pizza parlor, he asked Ammon if he wanted to get pizza and take it home for his siblings. The little boy nodded so hard Isaiah had to struggle not to laugh.

When they got out of the van, Ammon gripped Isaiah's hand as hard as he could. Clara opened the door to a space that resembled the medical clinic in Paradise Springs. She went to the desk to sign Ammon in and collected a clipboard with several pages on it.

Isaiah filled in what information he knew about the boy's health history as well as his parents'. Carrying it to the desk and paying for the office visit, he rejoined Clara and Ammon by a water dispenser that fascinated the little boy each time a bubble rose to the top.

An inner door opened, and a young woman in a pale yellow broadcloth shirt and jeans stepped out. She was almost as tall as Clara, but her hair, pulled back in a ponytail, was matte black. Walking to them, she said, "I am Trudy Littleton, one of the audiologists here." She spoke slowly and enunciated each word with care. "Are you Ammon?"

The little boy stared, then nodded.

She smiled and motioned for them to follow. Dr. Montgomery must have explained Ammon had lost his parents, because Trudy addressed Isaiah as "Uncle Isaiah." He'd have to thank the *doktorfraa* the next time he saw her.

First, Trudy led them to an examination room. She listened to Ammon's heart before peering into his ears and his throat.

"Everything looks normal," she said. "No signs of scarring or other injury in his ears. Let's see what else we can learn."

Again Ammon clutched his hand as Isaiah followed Clara and Trudy along a hallway. When Trudy opened a door at the far end of the hall, he saw the room beyond had a huge square cube to one side. The walls were covered with carpet. The single door had a tiny window, and another large window was at the far end by a simple table and chair.

"This is our testing facility," Trudy said. "It's sound-proof so we can measure what Ammon is hearing." She picked up a set of headphones and asked slightly more loudly and distinctly, "Do you know what these are, Ammon?"

He shook his head.

Trudy's smile returned. "A silly question for a plain boy, isn't it?" She set the headphones on her head, adjusting the earphones over her ears. "You wear them like this." Taking them off, she said, "When you go inside and wear these, I'll play music for you. When you hear it, I want you to raise your hand like this." She put up her right hand. "Then we'll play other games. Okay?"

Ammon glanced at Isaiah, abrupt fear in his eyes.

"Can I go in with him?" Isaiah asked.

"You may, but please don't give him any cues. We must determine what *he* can hear." She opened the door and motioned them to go in.

He heard her ask Clara to take a seat to one side before the door closed and sound cut off. The cube was lined inside with odd protrusions and more carpet. A pair of chairs was placed so the occupants could look out the window.

Trudy moved into sight, and a click resonated in the room. "If you want to sit and put on the headphones, Ammon, we'll get started."

Isaiah guided the little boy to a chair. Sitting him there, he put the smaller set of headphones hanging from hooks on the wall on Ammon. He took the chair next to the boy as Trudy explained over the loudspeaker that they'd start with tones.

Isaiah was amazed how tense he was as he watched the little boy raise and lower his hand. He saw Trudy's encouraging smile while Ammon didn't move; then the *kind* began saying words he must be hearing through the headphones. The words were random. Some came in quick succession while others seemed to have long breaks between them. He wondered what Ammon was hearing.

The speaker's click sounded again, and Trudy asked them to come out. She left Ammon with an aide in a nearby room filled with toys before, holding a manila folder, she led Isaiah and Clara to another door partway along the hall. Clara glanced at him, and Isaiah had to shrug. He had no idea what the tests had revealed.

The room had a desk and several chairs. The mini blinds at its single window were closed. The audiologist gestured for them to sit in two chairs by the desk. She went around to the desk and sat facing them. Opening the top drawer, she drew out a piece of paper. Graph blocks created a small rectangle on one side of the page. No marks had been made on it.

"This is the tool we use. It's called an audiogram," Trudy said, pointing to the graph. "When a patient is tested, the audiologist makes an X for the level of hearing in the left ear. We make a small circle for the level of hearing in the right ear. The numbers along the left side are for the horizontal lines and represent loudness. Quiet at the top and louder as the lines go down. We make the mark at the softest sound the patient hears at each note. The numbers along the top are for the nine vertical lines and have to do with the pitch of the sound. Each line from left to right goes higher in pitch. Think of it as a piano keyboard. The low notes are on the left, and the notes go higher as we go along the keyboard."

"What are the important numbers for Ammon to be able to hear?" Clara asked.

Trudy drew a box near the top of the audiogram and colored it in. "This is what's called the critical speech area. Pitches between 500 and 4000. For children, we like to see the loudness marks between 0 and 15. Anything in that box is considered good hearing. Do you have any other questions?"

Isaiah shook his head, not wanting his voice to crack with anxiety.

Beside him, Clara said, "I don't have any more questions."

"Good." Trudy opened the file folder and drew out a single sheet. She put it on the table between him and Clara. "Here are the results of Ammon's test. As you can see, your concerns about his hearing are justified."

He stared at the graph. A single X was drawn in the critical speech area. The circles ran across the bottom of the audiogram, and the other Xs were scattered between, though most were closer to the bottom than the top.

"Does this mean," Clara asked in a strained voice, "he can't hear much in his right ear?"

"If he can hear anything with his right ear," Trudy replied, "I'd be surprised. His hearing in his left ear is diminished. That he speaks so well is a blessing, but his speech will regress if his hearing isn't augmented. My suggestion is you have Ammon fitted for a hearing aid in his left ear as soon as possible. It'll allow the sounds he can hear to be amplified, especially in the critical speech area."

"What about his right ear?" Isaiah asked.

She sighed. "From the physical examination and the audio test, it's clear the nerves in his right ear are damaged. He can't hear vibrations in it. A hearing aid won't help. In fact, it might be detrimental because earwax can build up behind a hearing aid, and that could lead to ear infections."

"Do you think that's what caused the hearing loss?" He couldn't stop staring at the graph and the row of circles at the bottom.

"It's possible, though, as I said, I saw no signs of scars from multiple ear infections or any other damage caused by an injury. He may have been born with the nerves already defective." She gave them a sad smile. "There's no way to know without being able to talk to his parents. We need to work with what is and forget about what might have been."

"What do we need to do?" Clara asked.

"The first thing is to have him measured for a mold to make the hearing aid's insert for his ear. With your permission, I'll have my assistant do that."

The audiologist rose and left the room after Isaiah nodded, again not trusting his voice. Thank the *gut* Lord for Clara! She hadn't failed the boy.

Trudy returned and held out typed pages to him. "Here's basic information on the care and maintenance of a hearing aid. However, with a child Ammon's age, the most important thing is to get him accustomed to wearing it whenever he's awake. Be prepared. Some children resist because they hate having something in their ear or being teased. Others are bothered by the abrupt increase in what they can hear."

"His little sister has started wearing glasses." Clara chuckled. "She wasn't too happy, but Isaiah convinced her they were the very thing she needed. He can do that for Ammon, too, ain't so?"

He forced a smile as grief surged from his heart. He had no idea how to convince a five-year-old that wearing a hearing aid was no big deal. Glancing at Clara, who was asking more questions—ones he hadn't thought of— he knew he could depend on her to help him. Again he thanked God for sending her.

It's more than I deserve, he added, *but keep the twins in Your hands. They need You more because of my failures.*

He lowered his head, missing the closeness he'd once had with God. It was as if his prayers were having to rise to a very distant heaven instead of being heard by a loving parent who was never far away. He wished he could find his way to the relationship he'd had with God before Rose's death.

Trudy's voice intruded into his thoughts, and he looked up to see her holding out more papers, these folded into three parts. "These pamphlets will help you with making arrangements for him in the classroom as well as in other public places. The bottom one explains our payment plan for hearing aids. If you have any questions after you read them, please contact the office."

Isaiah took the pages numbly and was glad when Clara thanked the audiologist after Trudy asked them to return to the waiting room while they made the mold for Ammon's left ear. That way, she assured them, the hearing aid would fit when it arrived in a few weeks.

A few weeks? What if Melvin's parents or Esta's sister got to Paradise Springs before the hearing aid arrived? Would they be able to stay long enough for Ammon to get it, or would it have to be forwarded to where they lived?

Enough! He was worrying about inconsequential things. The family would want to help the *kinder*.

"Are you all right?" Clara asked as they sat on the chairs they'd used before.

"No."

"Me neither." She gave him a fleeting smile before lapsing into silence.

And there was nothing more to say other than how glad he was she was there with him. Those words he must keep to himself.

Chapter Twelve

Clara heard the rattle of buggy wheels on the stones in the lane and looked out the window. Isaiah! What was he doing at the house in the middle of the day? She wiped her hands on the dish towel and left the rest of the dishes soaking in the sink.

The twins were already swarming over Isaiah by the time she stepped outside. They greeted him with the same enthusiasm whenever he returned to the house, but they seemed a bit more excited than usual.

During the past two weeks, the days had flowed one into the other without much of note other than taking Ammon to Lititz to have his hearing aid fitted. The concerns he wouldn't want to wear it were for naught because he was delighted to be able to hear his siblings. It was the first thing he reached for in the morning and the last thing he took off at night. And Nettie Mae became less resistant to wearing glasses now that he had the hearing aid. Clara had warned them more than once that just because they had special tools to help them didn't mean they were any different from any other *kind* in the district. Each plain youngster had to learn being part of the community was more important than standing out.

As she neared, Isaiah went around to the back of his buggy and opened it. He pulled out bright blue pieces of plastic and black rods and netting. As he tossed each item on the grass, the twins became more excited.

"What's that?" Clara asked as he grabbed several of the larger pieces. She jumped aside when he dragged them past her.

"It's a trampoline. Or at least it's supposed to be once it's assembled." He dropped the pieces onto the ground not far from the sandbox and went to get more. When the twins picked up a few smaller parts near the buggy, he pointed to the spot where he wanted them put. "Daniel got it at the house where he's working. He's renovating a big farmhouse for an *Englischer* and his wife."

She glanced at the piles of parts on the grass. "They didn't want the trampoline?"

"No. From what Daniel told me, it was in the barn when his clients bought the house. Their *kinder* are grown, so they don't have any use for it. Daniel talked to them about the twins, and they decided to give him the trampoline for them."

"How generous!" She smiled. "It looks as if you've got your work cut out for you. There are a lot of pieces."

"Daniel is coming over later to help me put it together. He put one up for Joshua's youngsters last summer. He says he remembers most of the steps." He gave her a half smile. "Which is *gut* because we don't have any assembly instructions."

"I'll keep the kids away from it."

"You?" His smile broadened. "I'll watch them this afternoon."

"You aren't going to the forge?"

He shook his head. "I haven't taken as much time with the twins as I'd like. I want to while I can."

Clara blinked abrupt moisture from her eyes at the resignation in his voice. The *kinder*'s family could come at any time and take them, but they avoided speaking of it. Like the twins, they'd learned to pretend everything was fine.

"All right," she said. "I'll get supper ready."

"Or you could stay out here and work with us."

"I don't want to barge in on your time with them."

"How could you? You're part of their lives, too. Don't you want to help us? It'll be fun, Clara, and we could use fun in our lives."

The dampness in her eyes threatened to coalesce into tears. She blinked them aside as she nodded. He was right. She was taking everything too seriously.

"That sounds *wunderbaar*," she said, and took the hand he held out to her.

"C'mon!" he called to the twins. "Let's get this sorted out so we can put it together." As they began to try to figure out the pieces of the trampoline, she realized she'd forgotten how to have fun.

She didn't want to forget again.

By the time Daniel had arrived and they'd set to work assembling the trampoline, Isaiah was grateful for his younger brother's assistance. Clara excused herself to let them work and insisted the *kinder* go in the house with her so one of the heavier pieces didn't tumble on them.

It took them almost two hours to set up the trampoline and make sure it was safe. Isaiah was pleased when Clara and the twins reappeared as he and Daniel were putting away the last of the tools. She carried a pitcher of lemonade that was sweating as much as they were. The afternoon was humid, and thunderheads threatened over the western hills.

Taking a glass filled with ice and lemonade, he said, "Exactly what I was thinking about."

"I guessed." She smiled at the youngsters staring with delight at the trampoline. "The twins were eager to do something while they waited for you to finish, so we squeezed lemons." Looking at his brother, she added, "Daniel, would you like to join us for dinner?"

"*Danki*, Clara," his brother said after draining his glass and holding it out for a refill, "but I need to get home and help with Shelby's physical therapy. She won't let anyone else help her with practicing going up and down stairs."

"She's got *you* well-trained." Isaiah couldn't help envying his younger brother, who had fallen in love with a girl who came with a ready-made family.

"I'm wrapped around her little finger. Hers and Hannah's." Daniel finished his second glass of lemonade and handed it to Clara. He waved to them before heading to where his light brown buggy horse waited.

The *kinder* were clamoring to test the trampoline even before the buggy left. Cautioning them to put a big space between them so they wouldn't bump into each other, Isaiah lifted them, one after another, through the opening in the netting. As the trampoline shifted beneath them, they grabbed on to the netting and looked scared.

"Just bounce," he said.

Ammon did, jumping high and coming down hard. He fell to his knees and then flat on his face. He pushed himself up. The side of his face was reddened, but he was grinning.

"Bounce gently," Clara urged. "A little motion will make you go a lot." She grinned when the girls began to move with more confidence.

Soon all four *kinder* were leaping around the trampoline like mad rabbits. Their squeals of excitement were sweet music. Not quite laughter, but closer than he'd heard from them since that tragic night.

When the twins took a break to drink more lemonade, Isaiah asked, "Shall we try it, Clara?"

"You go ahead." She took a step away. "I should get dinner on the table."

"Not until you have your turn." He grasped her hands and tugged her forward.

"Clara's turn! Clara's turn!" shouted the twins, jumping with excitement as if still on the trampoline.

"You hear them." He yanked off his work boots and tossed them and his socks to one side. "They think it's a *gut* idea for you to take a turn." He grabbed her by the waist and lifted her onto the surface.

She gasped and clung to the netting to keep herself on her feet. "Give me a warning next time."

"I gave you one this time."

"Not much of one."

"But it was a warning." He swung up and began moving along the unsteady surface.

It was more fun than it looked, though it wasn't easy keeping his balance. Every downward motion seemed to create a stronger upward one. Starting slowly, he increased the pressure he put on the trampoline, jumping a bit higher each time. The twins cheered when he flapped his arms like a bird taking flight.

Spinning through the strengthening wind, which blew in heated gusts, he faced Clara. "You aren't jumping."

"I'm trying to stay on my feet. It's easier to give the twins advice than to do this myself."

"It's easier if you jump."

She laced the fingers of one hand through another section of the netting and held her *kapp* in place with the other as the wind swirled its strings across her cheeks. "I'll have to take your word for it."

He bounced hard, and she released the netting to throw out her arms to try to keep her balance. Grasping her hands, he pulled her to face him. "No, you don't."

"Isaiah! I'm going to break my neck!"

He halted his bouncing and steadied her as she was about to tumble off her feet. "Take it slow, Clara. You'll see how much fun it is."

"That's your opinion," she retorted, but gave him a saucy grin.

Again he began the slow, steady bouncing. He didn't release her hands as they went up and down together. Her grin became a gleeful smile when they bounced higher and higher.

"It's fun!" she shouted.

Thrilled he'd convinced her to toss aside her overwhelming sense of duty and enjoy herself, he looked into her pretty eyes that sparkled like ice in the pitcher. He was lost in their earth-brown depths. Hearing something like a heartfelt sigh, he wasn't sure if it came from his throat or hers. There was nothing in the world but the two of them and the slick surface of the trampoline beneath their bare feet.

As he thought that, he slipped when a gust of wind pushed him sideways. He fell forward but twisted to avoid hitting Clara. As he struck the trampoline, his breath bursting out of him, he realized she'd tumbled backward at the same time and had rolled out of his way. Before he could get to his feet, she'd crawled out of the trampoline and was standing on the grass, panting from exertion.

Isaiah climbed down, too, and she halted him from saying anything by pointing to the trampoline and shaking her head.

"I've learned my lesson," she said, leaning on the netting. "I'll leave this to you and the twins. This isn't something I can do by myself."

Ammon looked at her, as serious as a deacon scolding a member of the *Leit*. "In the Bible, it says, 'I can do all things through Christ which strengtheneth me.'"

She smiled. "It does, but I'm not sure if Paul had trampolines in mind when he wrote to the Phillipians."

"It means *all* things," the little boy insisted.

"He's right." Isaiah wasn't sure how much longer he could hold in his laughter at the little boy's attempt to reassure her. "It does say *all* things. We don't get to pick or choose."

Ammon nodded. "That's what *Mamm* says." Sudden tears flooded his blue eyes. "I miss *Mamm*. I miss her and *Daed*."

Gasps came from his siblings, and they frowned, wanting him to stop talking about their parents. Isaiah was too shocked to move, but Clara didn't hesitate. She went to her knees to wrap her arms around the *kind*. He threw himself against her and sobbed.

The other twins stared at Ammon, and Isaiah could see them struggling to contain their grief. It was impossible. One after another, their faces fell.

When Clara reached out and gathered Nettie Mae to

her, the little girl dissolved into sobs. Isaiah wrapped his arms around Nancy and Andrew. They cried, not like young *kinder*, but with the bone-deep weeping of someone far older who had suffered the worst blows life could bring their way.

An abrupt detonation of thunder followed a flash of lightning. He scooped up the little girl and boy and ran toward the house. Clara followed with Ammon and Nettie Mae. As soon as they entered the kitchen, all four *kinder* ran into the living room and crouched by the sofa, their heart-rending cries filling the silence between the rumbles of thunder.

"Go to them," Clara urged. "They need you."

"I don't know what to say to them." Something released inside him as he admitted he was at a loss for what to do.

"Say to them what you'd say to anyone else." She grasped his arms and looked at him. "Say to them what you wish someone had said to you when Rose died."

He stared, riveted by her advice. Why hadn't he thought of that himself? Many times, he'd wanted someone to sit and listen to him talk—or not talk—about Rose without telling him he was brave or he was strong enough to bear the burden of his loss.

He took one stiff step, then another toward where the *kinder* huddled together, looking for comfort from one another. Realization flashed like lightning through his mind. They believed they could find solace only from each other in their shared loss.

Sitting on the floor beside them, he didn't touch them. Instead he spread his arms in both directions along the sofa cushions, offering them an open invitation when they were ready. He wasn't sure if they were aware he'd come over to them because they hid their faces behind their hands or each other's shoulder.

"You know your *daed* and *mamm* would have come home to you if they could have, don't you?" he asked.

None of the youngsters replied, but they froze, and he knew they were listening to what he said. *God, please send me the right words. Let me be Your conduit to their hearts.*

"It's true," he went on aloud. "There's nothing your *mamm* and *daed* would have wanted more than to return to you."

"But they didn't!" The pain in Andrew's voice sliced through Isaiah, because he empathized with the boy. Being left behind by someone you love, especially when that person wouldn't have chosen to go, was agony.

"I know, and it hurts when I think about things I want to say to them."

"You too?" Nancy raised her head.

"All the time. Your *daed* was excited to see the gates when they were finished, and I couldn't wait to show him, but I couldn't. Not like I used to, but in my heart, I know he's near and celebrating with me."

"But," Nettie Mae said around a sob, "I talk. *Mamm* no talk. *Daed* no talk. Want to hear them!"

"Don't listen here." He pointed to his left ear before tapping the center of her narrow chest. "Listen here. In your heart."

"Where God is?" asked Andrew in awe.

"Ja." Envy struck him again, but this time for the boy's simple faith that hadn't wavered in the wake of his parents' deaths. He wished his had been as strong. Could it be again? All he needed to do was walk the path God had given him. Now wasn't the time to be thinking

of his troubles. He needed to help the twins, who were looking to him for help.

Clara stepped forward and sat on the other side of the *kinder*. She held out her arms, not saying a word. The girls launched themselves into her embrace. She held them close and comforted them. The boys inched nearer. She motioned for them to join in the group hug. Andrew and Ammon threw their arms around their siblings.

From the center of the hug, Clara began to sing *Jesus Loves Me*, and the youngsters joined one after another. When they stumbled on the *Englisch* words and looked ready to cry again, she switched to *Deitsch*. She began a different hymn when they finished, and the *kinder* sang until their tears stopped. She kept singing as the youngsters' eyelids grew heavy. While the twins fell asleep around her like a litter of puppies, she continued singing, making the hymns sound like both a prayer and a lullaby.

She extracted herself from among the *kinder* as the last one nodded off, worn out by the day's events and the release of the emotions they'd kept bottled up. Walking into the kitchen, she leaned her hands on the table and sighed. "I know I shouldn't pray for them to be able to set their grief aside because that would mean forgetting their parents. But for a few moments…" She glanced at him as he rose to follow her. "I'm sorry. I shouldn't have said that."

"It's fine. I know what you mean. It's not easy to walk between the *gut* memories and the grief. But it's a beginning for their healing."

"How about your healing, Isaiah? When is that going to start?"

Words failed him as he saw the sympathy on her face. There must be something he could say, but he had no idea what. As thunder crashed around them and wind-driven rain lashed the windows, the storm within him was louder. A calm would settle around the hills once the clouds passed, but it wouldn't be easy to quiet the turbulence inside him.

She raised a hand toward him, but he pushed himself away from the table and strode into the *dawdi haus*, shutting the door. He was as brittle as improperly tempered cast iron. If she touched him, he'd shatter as the metal would when struck by his hammer. He had no idea how he'd ever put himself together again.

Chapter Thirteen

Isaiah gave the long, flat piece of metal a final hit before putting it to one side rather than into the coals again. Stepping away, he wiped his forehead with the back of his hand. It was impossible to concentrate on work. He hadn't been prepared yesterday for the twins opening up about their grief over their parents' deaths. He was grateful for Clara's help as well as her pushing him to do what he needed to as the *kinder*'s guardian. But he kept hearing Clara's questions in his mind.

How about your healing, Isaiah? When is that going to start?

He should have answered her instead of walking away. He would have answered her if he'd known what to say. He'd wanted to say his healing was well underway, but he wouldn't lie. The more he thought about her penetrating questions that had stripped away the defenses he'd kept in place, the more annoyed he got. She didn't understand. Nobody did.

God does. The taunting, truthful voice in his mind burst out.

He ignored it as he tried to ignore Clara's questions. It was impossible.

The sound of a horse and buggy outside his smithy was a welcome respite from his thoughts. Or it was until he saw Curtis Mast step out of the buggy.

Isaiah silenced his groan as his father-in-law strode toward him. Forcing a smile, he called a greeting to Curtis.

"Busy?" the older man asked.

"Always, but being busy is better than not being busy, ain't so?"

Curtis nodded, then said, "I know it's not our way for a *daed* to interfere, but Ida Mae and I were wondering if we should plant extra celery in the garden this year."

The Amish tradition of serving celery at weddings demanded extra rows be sowed in the gardens of families expecting to host a wedding after the harvest. Any family who put in extra spent most of the summer warding off curious questions about which son or daughter was marrying and to whom. Only when the couple's intentions were published during announcements at a church Sunday service were suspicions confirmed or dashed.

But why was Curtis asking him?

"I don't have an answer for you," Isaiah said as he lifted off his leather apron and hung it on a hook beyond his forge.

"You haven't made your mind up yet?"

"Yet?"

"We're two grown men, Isaiah. You married one of my daughters. Don't you think, as part of the family already, you should let me know what your plans are since you're walking out with one of my other daughters?"

Isaiah opened his mouth, then shut it. He was too astonished and wasn't sure what to say. He tried again. "Did Orpha say…?"

"She hasn't said anything, but I've seen how she looks when she comes home late after walking out with you."

"I'm not walking out with Orpha."

"What?" Curtis's eyes grew as round as a coal on the forge.

"I don't know what she's said—"

"She hasn't said anything, which is why I assumed you two had reached a serious understanding." He tugged off his straw hat and rolled the uneven brim between his fingers. "So you're not walking out with her?"

"No. My time's spent here or with the Beachy *kinder*. Orpha must be walking out with someone else."

His father-in-law stared at him in disbelief, then sighed. "I'd hoped you would decide to marry her because I know you're a *gut* man who would provide a *gut* home for her. But apparently she's decided on someone else."

"It would seem so." His calm voice hid his exultation that Orpha wouldn't be pressuring him any longer to marry her. "It sounds as if congratulations will soon be in order, Curtis."

"Time will tell, but at least I know whoever she's with is plain because he drives a buggy. It's not like the bishop's Katie Kay who has jumped the fence to the *Englischers*."

"Is that for sure?" He couldn't ask Reuben, who must be torn up to have his daughter turn her back on her people.

And Micah… Isaiah wondered how his younger brother was dealing with these rumors. Micah had been busy on several construction projects, and Isaiah hadn't had much time to talk with him. He needed to make time.

Curtis shrugged, his mind on his daughters rather than the bishop's. "She's gone to live with an *Englisch* girl, so who knows whether she'll come back or not?" Putting his hat on again, he turned to leave. "If you hear who Orpha is spending time with, let me know."

The older man was gone before Isaiah could reply, which was just as well. No matter how bothersome Orpha had been, he wasn't going to carry any tales he heard to her *daed*. She was Rose's sister, and he owed her that much loyalty.

Clara had been delighted when Isaiah offered to bring pizza home for supper that night. It'd been such a treat when they'd had it after Ammon's hearing test, and the *kinder* would enjoy having it again. They'd been subdued, but brightened when she mentioned having pizza.

She wished the promise of pizza topped with pepperoni and mushrooms was enough to get herself on an even keel. Throughout the day, it was as if a shadow draped over her, something she hadn't experienced since her arrival in Paradise Springs. She wasn't sure if the shadow was from the storm of tears yesterday or if caused by the thunderstorms rolling through one after another during the afternoon. She was on edge.

But why? She should be rejoicing that the twins had realized it was okay to show their grief. It might be the first step toward convincing them to laugh again. But how could she revel in their breakthrough when Isaiah clung to his grief? She wished she could understand how he was able to offer the *kinder* what they needed when he refused to accept the same from her. Although she didn't want to believe what she could see, it seemed to her that he acted as if he deserved to be miserable. It made no sense.

Or did it? She'd been unhappy since she received Lonnie's letter. Only because she'd come to Paradise Springs and met Isaiah and the twins had she relearned how to smile and tease and enjoy simple, *wunderbaar* things.

Or maybe her uneasiness had nothing to do with him and the twins. Maybe it was from the two letters delivered that morning from the *kinder*'s grandparents. Like the one from their *aenti*, the letters were filled with news about where the couple was working in Africa. These had been written with the twins in mind, so she didn't have to edit as she read to them, but neither letter mentioned if or when their grandparents were coming to Paradise Springs.

How much longer would it be before they arrived? Clara had been at the Beachys' house for more than a month. She wasn't in a hurry to leave because she loved spending time with the twins. Having an hour in the evening to talk with Isaiah was a blessing, too, though she must make sure they didn't end up holding hands as they had on the trampoline. Had he guessed she'd stumbled because her knees had gone weak at his touch?

"You're wasting time better spent on doing something other than fretting," she chided herself.

While the boys played with their trucks and the girls with plastic horses they made gallop across the floor, Clara cut out clothes for the twins from the fabric she'd found in the other storage room upstairs. They were growing fast, especially the boys. They needed play clothes and nicer clothing to wear to services on a church Sunday. Today was a *gut* day to spend with the task because she could sit near the *kinder*, ready to offer a hug whenever it was needed, and not seem to be hovering.

The twins noticed what she was doing and asked which garment was for which *kind*. The girls were delighted with the light green and dark blue fabric she had for their dresses. As they wore the same size, they discussed which of them would wear which color first. The boys were less interested in color and more concerned that their new trousers didn't have hems halfway to their knees as youngsters their age often did, so new pants didn't need to be made every time they grew another inch. She assured them the hems wouldn't be any deeper than Isaiah's, but didn't mention why. With the *kinder* due to join their Mennonite relatives, their clothing could be quite different. She had no idea how conservative their *aenti* and grandparents were.

As the sky clouded for another round of thunder, lightning and rain, Clara put aside her sewing. The twins were getting antsy being stuck in the house, so she asked, "I've got my scissors out. Would you like me to cut your hair, boys?" She smiled at Andrew and Ammon. "Did your *mamm* cut your hair in the kitchen or bathroom?"

"Kitchen," Andrew replied, then lowered his eyes as he spoke about his *mamm*.

She guessed he didn't want anyone else to see tears in his eyes. Giving his shoulders a gentle squeeze, she wasn't surprised when he leaned into her instead of pulling away as he might have before yesterday. Perhaps now that they'd started to release their grief, they'd heal. It would take a very long time before the mention of their parents' names didn't cause pain. She hoped time would help reminiscences of the happy times eclipse their sorrow.

"*Mamm*'s shears here," Nancy said, opening the drawer

near the stove where Clara kept the matches and the other odds and ends needed in the kitchen.

"Gut." She reached in the drawer and pulled out the scissors. She also used a book of matches to light the propane lamp over the table as the clouds continued to thicken. Tossing the matches in the drawer, she closed it and said, "Please get me two bath towels, Nancy. You know how many two are?"

The little girl held up three fingers.

With a smile, Clara lowered one. "Put one towel on each of those fingers, and you'll have two towels. Nettie Mae, will you get a clothespin from the laundry basket?"

"One?" She held up a single finger.

"Perfect."

"What about me?" Ammon asked.

"You can help by getting one of the booster seats the girls use while Andrew pulls out the chair we'll use."

The *kinder* scurried in four different directions and did as she asked. Oh, how she was going to miss their eagerness to help! And their sweet smiles and their many questions. Tears welled up in her eyes, but she dashed them aside as she took the towels from Nancy. She put one on the floor and set on top of it the chair Andrew had moved away from the table. Ammon placed the booster seat on the chair.

When she motioned for him to climb up, Ammon scrambled like a squirrel climbing a tree. She wrapped the second towel around his neck and held it in place with the clothespin beneath his chin. After she had him hand her his hearing aid, because she didn't want to risk snipping its thin wire, she put it in her pocket for safe-keeping. She took a small mirror Melvin probably had used for shaving off the wall by the sink and handed it to the little boy.

"Be careful," she said.

"I will." His shoulders stiffened with his resolve.

The other *kinder* watched and chattered with each other and her as she cut Ammon's almost white hair. It was as fine as corn silk and clung to her fingers. She shook them to send the strands drifting to the towel on the floor.

The kitchen door opened, and Isaiah came in as Clara was finishing the last section of Andrew's hair.

"No pizza?" she asked.

"I thought we'd go to the pizza parlor and eat it there," he replied.

The twins cheered, and she had to put a hand on Andrew's shoulder to keep him from jumping like the others. She made the final snips before unhooking the towel from around his neck. "There." She shook the towel over the wastebasket, making sure the hair fell into it. "All done. As soon as I clean up, we can go for pizza."

"But what about *Onkel* Isaiah?" asked Ammon, who was talking more and more each day.

At that thought, she handed the device to him, and he slipped it into place with ease. It hid behind his ear and was almost invisible beneath his hair. More than once, she'd had to peer at him to make sure it hadn't fallen off.

"Aren't you going to cut his hair?" Ammon continued. "It's too long, too."

"Ja," interjected Nancy from where she was dancing around Isaiah with her twin sister. "Cut his hair, too! *Mamm* cut Andrew's and Ammon's and *Daed*'s."

The little girl halted as she mentioned her parents. Her face didn't crumble, but she was on the verge of tears. As she had with Andrew earlier, Clara put her arm around the youngster's thin shoulders and gave her a gentle hug. The little girl grabbed two handfuls of Clara's apron and pressed her face into it.

Knowing she needed to do something to lighten the mood in the kitchen, Clara asked, "Well, Isaiah, do you want me to cut your hair?"

Isaiah gave the slightest shrug, which meant the decision was in her hands. Hoping a quick trim of his hair would bring back the *kinder*'s *gut* spirits, she motioned toward the chair.

Andrew had already pulled the booster seat off it by the time Isaiah crossed the kitchen and sat. The twins gathered around the table to watch her cut his hair.

"Ready when you are," he said with a smile and a wink for the youngsters.

She hoped they'd giggle at him, but they only grinned. She had to be content with that.

Moving behind Isaiah, she listened to the twins tease him while she wrapped the towel around his shoulders and closed it with the clothespin. Where the towel had draped over the boys to their waists, it barely covered his broad shoulders.

She averted her eyes and picked up her scissors. "Your hair is longer than the boys' was," she said as she clipped and combed and cut more as he watched in the mirror to make sure his hair was the proper style and length set by the district's *Ordnung*.

"Getting my hair cut wasn't at the top of my list of priorities in the past few weeks."

"I know, but you don't want the deacon coming around to chide you for letting it grow to your shoulders."

He smiled. "You know if Marlin comes here, it won't be to chide me about my hair."

"True." His hair was almost as soft as the boys', but its color was much richer. "And it's true you'd do anything to avoid his matchmaking. Even let me cut your hair."

"You did a *gut* job with Ammon's and Andrew's, so why not?" He continued to tease her and the twins as she made sure his hair was even.

When she stepped around him to do the front, his gaze rose and locked with hers. Her fingers froze as she held a section of his hair between them. Had she believed cutting his hair would be no different from doing the boys'?

His almost gray eyes were unlike the bright blue of the *kinder*'s, but revealed so much more. The emotions within them were not the least bit childish. Nor was the tingling response his steady gaze created within her.

She dropped the hank of hair and started to move away. Gently he caught her wrist, keeping her where she stood.

"Don't," he whispered.

Don't what? Don't move away? Leave his hair half-cut? Look at him as if her heart was about to dance right out of her?

"Clara, it's okay." His quiet words wouldn't reach the twins, who'd gotten bored and gone to color in the living room. "We know where we stand." One corner of his mouth quirked, and she couldn't tell if he was trying to grin or trying not to. "Okay. Where you stand and where I sit."

She didn't smile as she finished trimming his hair. What would he say if she said her brain had lost complete control of her heart? She *knew* it would be foolish to fall in love with a man who had told her right from the beginning he didn't want to marry her. Hadn't she learned anything from her relationship with Lonnie?

But this was different.

With Lonnie, she had fallen hard and fast, but, in retrospect, she realized it hadn't been more than a crush and the opportunity to have a life with a man who appreciated her instead of believing she made a mess of everything, as her *daed* did.

But this love—and she couldn't pretend it was anything else—for Isaiah was real.

Utterly real.

Real and unrequited, and she was a fool to heed her heart when it was leading her to a grief greater than she'd ever known.

Chapter Fourteen

The news of an Amish family in a neighboring district needing money to pay for the hospital bills after the *daed* severed his finger while repairing a piece of equipment spread rapidly through Paradise Springs. His two sons had been in the field with him and had swiftly brought help, so there was hope the reattached finger could be saved. Isaiah heard about the accident the next morning when one of his regular customers came in to get his horses reshod. By the time he returned home that evening, Clara had learned about the tragic events from his *mamm*. Reuben had told her. The family of the injured man was in their bishop's other district.

By the next morning, someone had come to his brother's store with a stack of flyers announcing a chicken barbecue to raise money for the family. Amos put the flyers next to the cash register where everyone could see them, and he slipped copies into each bag of groceries when people checked out. The barbecue was going to be held at the school not far from where the man's family lived, about two miles from the Beachys' house.

Clara offered to bring her special potato salad along

with other favorite dishes, and Isaiah packed a dozen horseshoes for the men to enjoy tossing. The twins were excited to wear the new clothing she'd made for them, and Clara agreed, though the garments would come home with green splotches from playing in the grass. Vinegar would loosen the stains, and she'd made the blue dresses, dark pants and light green shirts as play clothes.

Isaiah hitched up Chip to the family buggy while Clara made sure the older twins were sitting as still as possible while they held covered dishes on their laps. The girls perched on the front seat between Clara and him. Nettie Mae held a package of napkins, and Nancy cuddled a plastic bag filled with paper cups. The youngsters looked serious about their obligations to get what they held to the school without letting it fall.

"All set?" he asked when Clara climbed in, tying her black bonnet over her *kapp*.

"*Ja.*"

"Checked the stove and the faucets?"

"*Ja.* I know the Bible doesn't say we're better safe than sorry, but it's something my *mamm* taught."

"Mine, too." He smiled as he slapped the reins on Chip, and they began driving toward the road.

As they approached the school, the road became crowded with buggies and cars and pickup trucks. It was like a mud sale but in the summer when nobody had to worry about ruining their shoes in the mire.

The aroma of chickens sizzling over a charcoal fire reached Isaiah before he drew the buggy to a halt. In spite of himself, his mouth watered. He hoped his stomach wouldn't grumble and embarrass him. Parking the buggy where a boy directed, he got out and helped Clara with the *kinder* before he went to unhitch Chip. The boy who was handling the parking wrote the number thirty-two on the side of the buggy with a piece of chalk, then marked Chip's halter with the same number before turning him out in a nearby field with the other horses.

By the time he was finished, Clara and the twins had vanished into the crowd. He hoped it wouldn't take too long to find them after he delivered the horseshoes to the near side of the school where they could set up a game. The *kinder*'s ball field was on the other side of the building, far enough away to keep everyone safe.

Isaiah drew in another deep breath of the delicious scent of cooking chicken and the unmistakable aromas of lemonade and chocolate. As soon as he found Clara and the *kinder*, they'd enjoy a *gut* meal.

He edged through the crowd, greeting those he knew and nodding to the people he didn't. His steps slowed when he saw Orpha standing by one table and putting out bowls of baked beans. She glanced at him, smiled and turned away to talk to Larry Nissley. Isaiah saw Larry was grinning like a fool. Larry must be the man walking out with Rose's sister. Orpha was quick-witted, and Larry was quick to speak before he thought. Theirs would be an interesting match, but he wished them well because they looked happy together.

"Having second thoughts?" Daniel and his twin brother Micah joined him. The two dark-haired brothers looked almost identical except Daniel had a cleft in his chin and Micah didn't.

Isaiah accepted the glass of lemonade Micah held out to him. "Second thoughts about what?"

"Orpha Mast. Word was going around you two would be making an announcement this fall."

"You know better," Isaiah said after he took a sip of the fragrant lemonade, "than to listen to rumors."

"I told you." Micah nudged his twin with his elbow. "Isaiah planning to marry Orpha was a rumor."

"But what about the other rumor?" asked Daniel, and his eyes began to twinkle.

"Which rumor would that be?" Isaiah enjoyed his brothers' teasing. Often when he saw Andrew and Ammon jesting with each other, he thought of how the Stoltzfus siblings always found ways to make each other laugh.

Laugh? How were they going to convince the Beachy *kinder* it was okay to laugh? He'd tried everything he could think of, and Clara had done the same, but the twins still refused to laugh. When asked why, their answer was the same. They'd been told not to laugh. Who could have done such a thing to young boys and girls?

"I'll give you a hint," Micah said. "Starts with *C* and sounds a lot like Clara Ebersol and you walking out together."

"Oh, no, not you too." He gave an emoted groan.

The twins exchanged a glance before Daniel asked, "Us too what?"

"Matchmaking."

Micah held up his hands. "Whoa there, big brother. All I did was ask if you'd heard the rumor about you two. A simple question."

Isaiah had to admit his brother was right. He apologized and added, "It seems anywhere I go with Clara and the *kinder*, someone is trying to make sure we spend time together."

"I thought you liked her." Daniel's dark brows lowered. "Is there some problem with her?"

"No. She's very nice, but nice isn't enough to base a marriage on."

"No?" Daniel began counting off on his fingers. "Ruth's husband, Elmer, is a nice guy. Joshua's Rebekah is nice. Ezra's Leah is nice. Amos's—"

Isaiah chuckled and held up his hands in surrender. "You don't have to go through the whole list of our siblings and their spouses to make your point."

"Gut."

"But in addition to being nice people, our siblings' spouses are in love with our brothers and sisters."

"And Clara is in love with you." Jeremiah, the brother who was a year younger than Isaiah, said from behind him.

Looking over his shoulder, Isaiah hid his shock. Jeremiah was the quiet one in their family. He spoke only when he believed he had something to add to the conversation. He was the least likely to try to get a rise out of someone or to tease them. If anyone in the family could be described as serious, it was Jeremiah. And Jeremiah was saying Clara was in love with Isaiah, as if it were the least unexpected news in the world.

"She loves the *kinder*, not me." Something sliced into his heart at his own words. "Once the twins' family comes for them, she'll head home. End of story."

"Stories often end with happily-ever-after." Daniel's smile broadened. Draping an arm over Jeremiah's shoulders, he said, "I saw ice cream being brought out. You know you'll want a sample."

Isaiah was relieved when the two walked away, but was surprised when Micah remained. He liked ice cream as much as Jeremiah did, and they'd often vied to see who could get the last spoonful out of the container.

He waited for his brother to say something, but when Micah remained silent, he asked, "How are you doing, Micah?"

"You know how you're annoyed about matchmaking?"

"Ja."

"That's how irked I get when someone asks me how I am. And there have been a lot asking since Katie Kay Lapp left the community."

"That's very irked."

Micah nodded. "Very, very irked."

"But how are you?" Isaiah asked, serious. "And I'm not asking because of Katie Kay."

"I'm fine, and that hasn't changed because she's gone. Katie Kay and I were something I thought might work out some day, but it's not going to happen."

"Sorry that—"

"Don't be sorry, Isaiah. I'm not." He winked and chuckled. "To prove that, I'll tell you that I've noticed Tillie Mast giving me the eye lately. Maybe I'll see if she needs a ride home tonight."

"Be careful with a Mast girl. Curtis and Ida Mae are ready to marry them off to anyone who looks at them twice."

Micah laughed and slapped him on the shoulder. "Look who's talking. The man everyone is talking about. They're interested in whether you'll marry Orpha or Clara by year's end. I've been asked about that close to a thousand times."

"You're exaggerating."

"Ja, but not by much. Hey, it's my turn to toss horseshoes. See you later, bro."

Isaiah smiled as his brother crossed the schoolyard to where the horseshoe games were underway. Micah had picked up a lot of *Englisch* slang while working on various construction projects with *Englischers*.

Where were Clara and the twins? The crowd seemed to be growing by the minute, and he wanted to make sure those hungry youngsters got fed before the food was gone.

When he found them, the boys were already discussing if they wanted their chicken with the barbecue sauce or without. The girls were more interested in the pretty cakes set in a row on a pair of tables. They smiled, along with Clara, when he suggested they join the line waiting to select what they wanted.

It took him and Clara as well as Neva Fry to get their six plates from the serving line to one of the blankets spread on the grass. He thanked the schoolteacher, who waved and hurried to help other parents with more *kinder* than hands to load and carry plates.

They enjoyed the delicious meal, and he smiled when the boys asked about getting seconds. Nobody left hungry from an Amish fund-raising meal. He went with the boys to get more chicken and sides. Though he wondered how they'd eat everything, their plates were soon clean again.

"Why don't we walk around a bit before dessert?" Clara asked when the twins began to discuss which sweets they wanted. "Let what we've eaten settle a bit."

"The best idea I've heard in a long time." Isaiah pushed himself to his feet and smiled as he offered his hand to help her up. When she smiled and let him take her hand, his heart felt lighter than it had in longer than he could recall. Though she withdrew her fingers from his as she turned to help the *kinder* pick up their plates and forks so they could carry them to one of the long plastic washtubs, she wasn't scurrying away as she had before.

He was too aware of her fingers close to his as they walked side by side among the crowd. He itched to grasp hold of her slender hand, but he couldn't be unaware of the eyes following them and the twins. Giving the rumors substance would be the worst thing he could do for her, the twins and himself. Clara would be leaving once the *kinder* were settled. He couldn't forget that, but he also knew he'd never forget her.

"Isaiah, can I talk to you for a moment?" came an all-too-familiar voice from behind him.

He turned to see Orpha. "Certainly."

"If you'll excuse us," Clara began, reaching to herd the twins away.

Orpha put out her hand. "No, please stay, Clara. You should hear this, too."

When Clara bent and whispered something to the twins, they nodded and scampered away toward where his *mamm* was putting plates of cookies and sliced pieces of pie on a folding table. Isaiah smiled, realizing Ammon had been able to hear Clara's soft voice as the others did. What a blessing she'd been in the *kinder*'s lives as well as in his!

"I don't want to keep you, but I do want to say I'm sorry." Orpha rubbed her hands together as she looked from him to Clara. "I shouldn't have taken out my frustration with my parents on the two of you. Neither of you have been anything but kind to me." She turned to Clara. "What you said at Hersheypark about spreading vitriol made me realize how I was making you into scapegoats. *Danki* for the reminder that our Lord taught us to treat each other as we'd want to be treated. And I wasn't, but I'm going to try harder to do that."

"*Danki*, Orpha," she said. "I know it isn't easy for you to say this."

"It isn't, but it's easier than it would have been if I hadn't discovered what love is. Real love." She glanced toward where Larry was pretending not to be watching them. Averting her eyes, she said, "I'm not sure where discovering love will take me. Or when, but I know I'd be foolish to settle for anything less than true love." A sad smile edged along her lips. "Rose told me that. I hope you'll forgive me."

"You know we already have," Isaiah replied as Clara nodded beside him. *Now if I could forgive myself.* He was glad those words were only in his mind. They sounded pitiful and complaining…and they were. Why wouldn't his thoughts heed him? Forgiveness was necessary if one wanted to be closer to God.

Did he want to keep a space between him and God? Like Orpha's anger being spewed at him and Clara, it was the easy way out. But not God's way for him.

His eye was caught by Reuben coming to stand beside *Mamm*. She laid a gentle hand on his sleeve. She left it there for the length of time it took Isaiah to blink, but he couldn't miss the way the bishop slanted toward her. The two motions were as loud as a shout.

Reuben and *Mamm* were falling in love. No, he corrected himself. They *were* in love. Their second chance at a once-in-a-lifetime love, a true gift from God. He looked to where his oldest brother Joshua sat with his family and his second wife. Joshua had been granted that *wunderbaar* gift also.

He heard his brothers' voices echoing from his memory. They'd believed Clara was in love with him. Was it possible for him to receive the same blessing?

Ja, came the soft voice of his conscience. *It's possible because you've already been blessed with the second chance.*

He watched Clara assisting the twins to carry their desserts. Dear, sweet Clara who had set aside her life to come to help him and the *kinder.* She loved the twins without reserve, but, as he'd sensed almost from the beginning, she held back a part of herself from everyone else, including him.

Had God brought her into his life to help him see he could trust the path set out for him? Or was Isaiah supposed to help *her* heal? It was an unexpected thought and a startling one he needed to consider and pray about, because he'd never guessed that helping her might be the way to help himself.

Clara swung Nancy's and Nettie Mae's hands as they stood in line to wait for ice cream. The little girls bounced from one foot to the other and chattered like squirrels as they discussed which flavor to pick. With the choice of chocolate, chocolate peanut butter, strawberry and vanilla, it wasn't an easy decision. In addition, they could select chocolate sauce or crushed pineapple to go on top of their scoops.

"What you want, *Aenti* Clara?" asked Nancy.

"I'm trying to decide between strawberry and vanilla."

"Want chocolate," Nettie Mae announced, and people around them grinned.

"Me, too." Nancy paused, then added, "But peanut butter, too."

That set off another round of discussion between the little girls. Clara listened with a smile. The conversation would keep them busy while the line inched forward.

Scanning the crowd that had grown larger, she knew the injured man's family would be grateful for the generosity of those who had donated food and come to share it and time with each other. Clara recognized many people, but more she didn't. She wondered if the unfamiliar plain folks were from Reuben's other district. A lot of *Englischers* had come to the chicken barbecue, as well. She'd met a few of them at Amos's store or around Paradise Springs, but most were strangers.

A gasp caught in her throat as she stared at a man striding through the crowd as if he were the host of the gathering. It wasn't possible, was it? She found him again among the crowd. Her eyes weren't fooling her. Nobody walked through a crowd as Floyd Ebersol did. His head was high, and his eyes scanned those around him as if looking for someone. But she knew the truth. He was keeping track of those who watched him.

Pride was an abomination to the Amish, but not her *daed*. He wanted to be the center of attention wherever he went. More than once, he'd said he hoped the lot would fall on him, so he could serve as an ordained minister or deacon. He'd admitted to aspiring to be a bishop, though she doubted he could be as humble as their bishop or Reuben Lapp was.

She looked around, but didn't see her *mamm*. It wasn't a big surprise, because *Mamm* had seldom left the house since she'd broken her hip. She now walked with a painful limp. Many times Clara had wanted to ask her *mamm* if she stayed in the house, except for chores, because *Daed* didn't want to share any attention with her. Clara prayed it wasn't because her *daed* deemed *Mamm* unworthy of being seen with him because she hobbled.

Reaching the front of the line, she focused on helping

the girls order their ice cream. She shook her head when asked if she wanted some, too. She couldn't imagine putting anything in her roiling stomach. As she turned to lead Nancy and Nettie Mae to a spot where they could eat their ice cream before it melted on their clothes, she saw her *daed* walking in her direction with a determined expression.

"Go and sit with the boys," she said to the twins. "I'll be there in a minute."

With grins already colored pink and brown from their ice cream, the two girls obeyed. She watched, and they'd reached the boys just as her *daed* stopped in front of her.

"Clara," he said as a greeting.

"How are you doing, *Daed*? Is *Mamm* here? I didn't realize you were coming. You should have…" Her voice faded when his brows lowered in his customary frown. This time she deserved his silent censure. She'd been babbling.

"I hear you're being courted by a minister." He didn't let her reply before he said, "Of course, you must not make a mess of this as you did with Lonnie Wickey."

Reminding her *daed* that nothing she'd done had led to Lonnie marrying another woman would be a waste of breath. "No," she said in the calmest tone she could muster, "I'm not being courted by a minister. Isaiah Stoltzfus, who is the guardian of the *kinder* I'm taking care of, is a minister, it's true, but we aren't walking out together."

"You should encourage him. A minister would be a *gut* match for you, and as a widower, he must be eager to wed and would likely overlook what happened with your previous betrothal."

Clara was shocked speechless. In spite of his chiding

about her shortcomings, she hadn't expected her *daed* to think her unworthy of being loved for herself.

"Floyd Ebersol?" asked Isaiah from behind her.

She closed her eyes. How much of her *daed*'s comments had he overheard? She wished the ground would open right where she stood and swallow her.

"Ja?" *Daed* squinted at Isaiah. Did he need glasses as Nettie Mae did? If he thought they made him look old or less dignified, he'd eschew them as the little girl had tried to. "You are?"

"Isaiah Stoltzfus." He smiled as if no tension hung in the air. "I want to tell you, Floyd, that your daughter has been a blessing. She has been a great help with the twins. *Danki* for allowing her to come and help us. Her kindness toward us speaks well of her upbringing."

Clara was astonished as Isaiah continued, saying what *Daed* would want to hear. Each time Isaiah praised her, he made it sound as if her *daed* was the reason she'd done well. In a way, it was true, because she'd treated the twins as she'd prayed he would treat her. With love and understanding instead of impatience and unreasonable expectations.

Her *daed* preened, accepting Isaiah's words as his due, and he smiled when Isaiah said, "I'm sorry to take Clara away from you, but we need to check on the twins."

"Of course." He waved them away.

Clara kept her feet from sending her running away at top speed. Instead, she walked beside Isaiah. When he glanced over his shoulder, she did the same and saw her *daed* talking with another man.

Isaiah grabbed her arm and pulled her behind the school. Sitting her on the back steps, he sat beside her.

She started to rise, saying she had to check on the twins, but he halted her.

"Leah and Mandy are watching them. They'll be fine." He brushed a strand of hair from her face. "But what about you? How are you?"

"I'm okay, too."

"You looked pretty upset, so I decided to butt in. I figured I owed you for when you saved me from Orpha's machinations, but I was surprised when someone said the man you were talking to was your *daed*."

"Danki." She looked at her folded hands. If she said more, the jagged tears in her throat might burst out in sobs.

"Be honest with me, Clara."

"I am."

He shook his head. "Not about why seeing your *daed* upsets you."

Raising her head, she asked, "How much did you hear of what he said?"

"Not much. With everyone around, it's hard enough to hear myself, let alone anyone else." He put one hand over her clasped hands. "What are you afraid I heard?"

"Not afraid. Ashamed."

"Ashamed? You? Clara Ebersol, you're the most loving, generous person I've ever met. You've put your life on hold to help strangers with bereaved *kinder*, and you've helped those *kinder* begin to heal. What could a person like you be ashamed of?"

She should put a halt to the conversation, but her heart demanded to unburden itself to someone she could trust. "My *daed* expects me to be perfect."

"Nobody is perfect."

"Floyd Ebersol's daughter must be. He won't let me

forget what he sees as my greatest failure because he believes it reflects on him, too."

"What failure?"

Clara plunged into the story of how she'd been courted by Lonnie Wickey, the promises made and the promises broken. It took less time to tell than she'd guessed.

"But where did *you* fail?" Isaiah asked when she was done.

"I failed in my *daed*'s eyes by humiliating my family. I wish I could make him see I never want to do anything to hurt him and *Mamm*."

He lifted her hands between his and sighed. "There are some battles you'll never win."

"So I should give up?"

He shook his head. "No, but you should accept what's impossible to change. And it appears your *daed* is one of those unchangeable parts of your life."

"*Danki*, Isaiah. I guess I've got a lot of lessons to learn."

"All of us do." His gaze searched her face, and she wondered what he was looking for and if it was there. "We need to keep learning until we take our last breath because life is challenging."

"How did you get so wise?"

"Hard lessons." He released her hands and framed her face with his large hands.

His mouth found hers, silencing any protests before they could form, though she didn't want to be anywhere but with him. His kiss was gentle, and she curved her arms around his shoulders as he deepened the kiss until quivers rippled through her. How could she have thought his kiss would be like anyone else's? It was beyond *wunderbaar*.

When he raised his head, she remained where she was. She traced one of his pale brows with a single fingertip. He smiled before pressing his lips to her palm. That was sweet, but not what she yearned for. She drew his mouth to hers. He held her close until she couldn't guess if the frantic heartbeat was hers or his.

He lifted his mouth away again. This time abruptly. The softness vanished from his face as dismay filled his eyes. Standing, he didn't look at her. "I'm sorry, Clara. I shouldn't have done that."

She didn't rise as she wrapped her arms around herself, fearing she'd fall to pieces in front of him. Sorry? Did he mean kissing her was a mistake?

Fool! That's what you are. A second man is saying he made a mistake after he kissed you!

"Don't worry, Isaiah," she said, staring at the ground. "It won't change anything." Her words were the truth. She'd felt like an idiot when she came to Paradise Springs because she'd fallen for a handsome man who acted as if he loved her. When she left Paradise Springs, she'd feel the same way…for a different handsome man.

No, this pain was far deeper because her love for Isaiah was far stronger than anything she'd experienced with Lonnie.

The shadow of his hand moved toward her, then jerked away. She closed her eyes, but the sound of his steps disappearing around the side of the school were like blows against her heart. She hung her head and wept.

Chapter Fifteen

Before the week had passed, Clara knew her plan to avoid Isaiah until the twins' family came for them was doomed to failure. They had to share meals and taking care of the *kinder*. When he closed the door connecting the main house to the *dawdi haus*, she remained as aware of him as if the walls had become transparent. And the twins talked about him. Their affection for him had not changed.

Nor had hers, and that was the problem. Too often, the remembered sensations of his lips on hers played through her mind. Those memories urged her to toss aside caution and risk her heart again.

Isaiah had been very clear—right from the beginning—he wasn't ready to marry again. He'd been honest when he told her that his focus had to remain on his obligations. Even their *wunderbaar* kisses could not deter him from doing as he must. He couldn't let his work at the forge slide, because too many local people depended on him to shoe their horses. He never would shirk his duties as a minister. Nor would he do less than everything he could to take care of the *kinder*.

Despite knowing that, she'd followed her heart to him. She'd been foolish with him as she'd been with Lonnie. More foolish, because she should have learned from her earlier mistakes. She could forgive her *daed* for his pride, but would *Daed* forgive her if he believed she'd destroyed another opportunity to marry well?

Hochmut. Her *daed* had too much of it; yet she would never change him. Isaiah was right.

She needed to concentrate on changing her heart, which refused to heed anything but its yearning for Isaiah. She needed to follow Isaiah's lead and concentrate on something other than being in love with him. Looking around the house, she sighed. The floors were swept. The dishes were done. Dinner was ready to be cooked. The *kinder* were playing quietly upstairs. She'd weeded the garden that morning. She could start the laundry, but it was too late in the day for it to dry before night fell. Maybe reading would help. She hadn't had time since she'd arrived, and she'd packed a book, planning to finish it while in Paradise Springs.

Going to her room, she edged around her bed. She picked up the book from the table where she'd stacked the few things she'd brought with her. She gasped when something fell out. An envelope. She recognized it, though she couldn't recall putting the letter in the book.

Opening the envelope, she drew out the single page as she sat on the edge of her bed. She read the words she'd read dozens of time already. The letter was from Lonnie, the last one he'd written her to let her know he was sorry about how things had turned out. He confessed he'd believed he loved her, but he'd discovered what love was when he met the woman who became his wife. He'd never wanted to hurt Clara, but he had to follow his heart.

Giving up the love he'd found and honoring his offer of marriage to Clara would have led to them being miserable the rest of their days.

She looked at the final paragraph. Her eyes filled with tears that blurred the words that she hadn't truly understood until now:

> Clara, I treasure the time we shared, and I hope some day we can view that time with smiles and know what we shared was part of our journey to true and lasting love. I wish for you what I've found. You deserve someone who will make you happy instead of just content.

Lowering the page to her lap, she whispered, "I'm sorry, Lonnie. I've been blaming you for what happened exactly as my *daed* blamed me. What happened was nobody's fault. You fell in love with someone else. You couldn't help what your heart wanted, and, if I'd cared about you as much as I should have, I would have been happy for you. And for me, because you're right. I didn't love you, and you didn't love me enough."

She closed her eyes. She could finally look beyond her wounded pride to the truth. But had she learned to listen to *gut* sense? No! If her rational side had its way, she wouldn't be listening to her heart, which drew her to Isaiah.

Sounds came from the twins' room, and she folded the letter and put it in its envelope. "Goodbye, Lonnie," she whispered. "I hope you're always as happy as you deserve to be."

Clara didn't have any more time to think about the letter and her realizations about herself because the *kinder* seemed more wound up than usual. They ate their after-noon snack so quickly she wondered if they even tasted the chocolate chip cookies. She was glad to shoo them outside to play while she cleaned up from their snack. But first she wanted to check on the mail and any mes-sages on the answering machine. She'd been sure that they would have heard from the twins' family by now.

No light blinked by the phone in the shack by the road, and the only mail was a blacksmithing supply catalog for Isaiah. She carried it to the house and put it on the kitchen table. Picking up the dishes left by the twins, she filled the sink with soapy water.

She used to put his mail beside where he sat in the liv-ing room in the evening, but now he rushed to the *dawdi haus* before the twins went to bed. She half expected him to take his plate and eat in the other part of the house one of these nights. The *kinder* had begun to ask why he wasn't spending more time with them.

Everything they'd built for the twins was falling apart. The sooner the *kinder*'s family returned and could start the youngsters on their new life, the better it would be for everyone.

Oh, how she wished she could believe that! The thought of not seeing them every day cramped her heart. She couldn't think about never spending time with Isaiah again. If she did, she wasn't sure she could continue with their tacit agreement to pretend nothing had changed.

A motion caught her eye, and she looked out the win-dow. A half scream burst from her throat when she saw smoke was curling out of the stable window. Fire!

She threw the dishcloth in the sink and raced out the back door. Where were the *kinder*? They'd been in the yard moments ago.

Screaming their names, she grabbed the garden hose. It was too short. It'd never reach the stable. She needed to call for help. But she couldn't when she didn't know where the twins were. She shrieked their names again, scraping her throat raw.

Andrew burst out of the gray cloud. He yelled for help. She grasped his shoulders and shook him to reach past his terror.

"Where are the others?" she asked.

He pointed at the stable.

"Go and call the fire department," she ordered as she gave him a shove toward the phone shack. "Call 911! Tell the firemen to come right away. Can you do that?"

"Ja." His voice trembled on the single word.

"Go!"

She ran to the stable. A single glance over her shoulder told her Andrew was speeding toward the end of the farm lane as fast as his legs could pump. She hoped he could do what she'd asked. If he couldn't, she'd have to make the call herself.

After she made sure the *kinder* and her horse were out of the burning building.

The smoke met her at the door. Hot and smothering and as solid as a wall, it tried to drive her back from the fire's domain. She pushed forward. Holding her hands over her nose and mouth, she scanned the stable. Thick smoke hid the ceiling and reached almost to the floor. She heard her horse moving in panic.

Clara lowered her hands enough to cry out, "Ammon!" *Oh, dear Lord, let him be able to hear me!* "Nancy! Nettie Mae! Where are you?"

She heard muffled sobs. The stall in front of her on her right side. Holding her apron over her nose and mouth,

she ran in. She almost tripped over two small forms huddled in one corner beside a bale of hay.

"Clara!" they called together, jumping to their feet.
Nancy and Nettie Mae!

"Is Ammon with you?"

The girls looked at each other but didn't answer.

She knelt and grasped each one by the shoulder. Closer
to the floor, the air wasn't as thick with smoke. She sent
up a grateful prayer as she repeated her question. When
the girls hesitated, she hurried to say, "We need to get
out of here."

Rising, she pushed them ahead of her to the door. She
shoved them out and gasped a deep breath of the fresher
air. Again she asked them where Ammon was.

Both girls shrugged, their eyes wide with terror.

Telling them to go to the front porch and wait there,
she turned to head back in. Where should she look?
Flames were licking along the eaves. She wouldn't have
much time to find the little boy.

A small hand tugged her skirt before she could move.
Nettie Mae!

"Ammon hiding, too," the little girl said.

"Where?"

"He not mean to—"

"I know he's sorry." She didn't have time for the *kind*
to explain. "But where is he? Do you know?"

"He love Bella."

Clara hoped she was translating the little girl's cryp-
tic statement. Ammon had gone to rescue her horse. If
she was wrong, she wouldn't have another chance. Even
if she was right…

She told Nettie Mae to join her sister on the front
porch. Hoping the *kind* obeyed, she ran into the smoky

stable. It was the hardest thing she'd ever done, but getting out alive with Ammon was going to be more difficult.

Isaiah heard a fire alarm rise to an ear-piercing pitch. It was the one belonging to the Paradise Springs Volunteer Fire Department in the center of the village. He dropped his hammer and yanked off his leather apron. He banked the embers on the forge, then raced around the building between him and the parking lot. He didn't slow until he reached the road.

As he got there, the main fire engine zipped past, followed by trucks and cars driven by volunteer firefighters. A red pickup slowed long enough for him to hold out his hands to the three men in the back. Two plain and one *Englischer*, he saw as he swung up beside them. The truck took off after the fire engine before his feet touched the truck bed.

Dropping beside the men amid the piles of gear labeled PSVFD, he asked, "Where's the fire? Is it a building?"

As one, they shrugged. The *Englischer* explained they'd been working nearby and reached the fire station in time to see the fire engine race out. They'd grabbed the rest of the turnout gear and jumped into the red pickup without asking questions.

Awkwardly each man found gear and pulled it over his clothes. Isaiah didn't bother with boots, because he wore protective ones in the blacksmith shop, but he helped others find ones that fit.

A shrill screech came from behind the vehicle. A police car was catching up with them. Following it was an ambulance. His stomach clenched. His hopes that it was nothing but a grass fire were dashed. Was it a car accident?

Please don't let it be that, God. The twins were too fragile to deal with more funerals.

He heard a curse and a prayer. He looked at the other men, not sure which had said which. Then he noticed where the truck was turning and looked along the familiar road to see a plume of smoke rising in malevolent blackness less than a half mile away.

He started to stand to see better. He was grabbed and pulled down.

"It's the Beachys'!" someone shouted.

He shook off the hands but didn't stand. He couldn't risk his life. Not when Clara and the twins could be in danger. Groaning, he hid his face in his hands.

Don't let me to be too late again! Let me be there in time this time!

The prayer played over and over in his mind as he raised his head to see the fire engine race past the house. He sent up a quick prayer of thanksgiving. He saw motion on the front porch. One…two…three… Where was Ammon? And where was Clara?

He knew the answer when he saw flames stretching out a stable window. Clara was wherever Ammon was. If the boy was in the stable, she'd be there, too.

Help us, Lord! Don't let me be too late. Not this time. Not for them.

The pickup squealed to a halt, and Isaiah jumped out. He heard buggy wheels clattering behind him as help arrived from neighboring farms. Orders were being shouted in every direction as the firemen hooked a hose to the pumper and ran another line toward the pond beyond the big barn.

Isaiah ran toward the stable. He heard shouts behind him, but he didn't stop. If Clara and the boy were inside, they didn't have time to wait for the firemen to finish getting their hoses ready. Suddenly the oft-heard jest that the Paradise Springs Volunteer Fire Department had never failed to save a foundation was no longer funny. Things could be replaced but not people.

That was a lesson he'd learned over and over, and he didn't want to be taught it again today.

"Clara! Ammon!" he shouted as he pushed through the smoke trying to force him back.

The flames roared like a tormented beast from the far end of the building. If a spark flew to the main barn, that could be destroyed, too. He hoped the cows had the sense to move away. The chickens would be hiding closer to the house.

But Clara wouldn't go to safety until the *kinder* did.

He shouted their names to his right.

No response.

He drew in a deep breath to shout them again, then began coughing as the smoke choked him with its gray, cloudy fingers.

A hand grasped his.

Clara!

He didn't know if he said it aloud or not, but he pulled her toward him. His arm went around her slender waist. He could feel her straining to breathe.

"Ammon?" he shouted over the ear-shattering crackle. This blistering beast was nothing like the fire he controlled on his forge.

"Out."

"I didn't see him."

"He's out."

"Then let's get out, too!"

"Bella!" she choked, pulling away from him.

Or at least he thought she said that. The swirling smoke swallowed her before she'd gone more than a couple of steps. He followed, glad he could turn away from the most vicious heat.

He heard her horse before he could see Clara and Bella through the smoke. The horse was pushing against the stall, seeking any way out—though, he knew, if the door was open, Bella might not flee. Thick smoke mixed with fear scorched a horse's brain, making it impossible for one to escape.

Grabbing a smoking blanket off a stall door, he dunked it in the watering trough. He heaved it over Bella and grabbed her mane. She tried to pull away, but he shouted for her to come with him. Pulling her out, he looked for Clara.

He couldn't see. Anything. The smoke was growing blacker by the second, and his eyes burned as if twin pyres had been lit in them. He groped for the other stall. The crackling of the fire had become a roar that swallowed his shout.

He bumped into something soft. Clara! Coughing and gagging, she leaned against the stall door.

He seized Clara by the waist and tugged on Bella. Bending his head as if he strode through a storm wind, he gulped in the cooler air toward the floor while he rushed toward the door. He herded her before him. Bella followed, shying on every step.

Overhead something creaked. Were the rafters failing? If the roof collapsed, they'd be crushed.

Then fresh air filled his lungs. He started to cough, but kept moving forward. Water sprayed over them. It was aimed at the stable, but the mist was icy cold after the inferno inside. Shouts came from every direction, but he couldn't sort them out. Bella pulled away and galloped around the house and out of sight.

Small forms ran toward him and Clara, who leaned more heavily on him with each step. Arms reached out to catch the youngsters before they could get too close to the fire. He hurried Clara toward the twins.

They threw their arms around him and Clara. As he released her to hug them, she collapsed to the ground and didn't move. The twins shrieked in terror.

He wanted to as well, fearing, once again, he'd been too late. He dropped to his knees beside her and moaned, "Don't leave me, Clara. Lord, don't take her, too. Please."

Chapter Sixteen

Isaiah watched the other firemen putting out the last of the hot spots around the stable as he paced between the house and the fire engine. The captain had refused to let him fight, telling him he was too emotionally involved. He'd proved it by rushing into the stable. That everyone, including Bella, had been saved was no justification for what he'd done. Isaiah knew the captain would have more to say once the cleanup was done, and he would accept whatever punishment the captain handed out. He'd let his fears overcome his training, and he could have endangered his fellow firefighters if they'd had to come to his rescue.

The stable was a scorched skeleton of timbers. The building had been too involved by the time the firefighters arrived. However, other than smoke stains, the larger barn was undamaged and the animals, except a few chickens, were safe. The missing chickens would likely reappear when they were hungry.

Isaiah had no idea how the fire started. He was careful. He didn't leave a lamp in the stable, not wanting one of the horses to bump into it and tip it over. Maybe the *kinder* had seen something. He gave them a quick hug before *Mamm* appeared and took them into the house. At the same time, the EMTs had rushed Clara into the ambulance to work on her. They'd told him to wait outside, out of the way.

Glancing at where the ambulance stood in the yard, he had to believe the fact it hadn't rushed off to the hospital meant she was going to be okay. She had to be okay. He couldn't bear the thought of another woman he loved dying.

Ja, he loved her. With his defenses seared away, he couldn't ignore the truth any longer. He loved Clara Ebersol. He loved her magnificent red hair and her snapping eyes that mirrored her emotions, whether she wished them to or not. He loved her sense of humor and her sense of duty with the *kinder*. He loved her faith that was as much a part of her as her scintillating smile. He loved her courage and her weaknesses, including the one she never spoke of: her fear she wasn't *gut* enough to meet anyone's standards, including her own.

He loved *her*.

And he wanted to tell her how wrong her fear was. She was the most *wunderbaar* woman he'd ever known.

Isaiah paused in his pacing when Finn Markham approached him. The EMT was also a member of the Paradise Springs Volunteer Fire Department, and Isaiah had worked with him on several occasions. He'd never thought he'd need the tall *Englischer* in his official capacity.

Finn clapped a hand on his shoulder. "Good news, Isaiah. Clara is breathing well on her own."

"Will she have to go to the hospital?"

"Her blood oxygen levels are low, but that's to be expected. We'll check again in a half hour. If they've stabilized, she won't have to go."

"Can I see her?"

"I don't think I could stop you." Finn gave him a bolstering smile. "She's been asking about you and the children. We've tried to reassure her that you're all okay, but I don't think she'll believe that until she sees you with her own eyes."

"I'll get the *kinder*."

Putting a hand on Isaiah's arm, the EMT said, "It'd be better right now if it's just you. She's pretty weak. She breathed in a lot of smoke, and it'll be a few days before she's 100 percent again. The kids may get her too excited, and that's going to have an impact on her oxygen levels."

"All right." He took one step, then stopped. "*Danki*, Finn. I owe you a debt I'll never be able to repay."

"Have your mother make me one of her *snitz* pies, and we'll call it even."

"If I know *Mamm*, she'll make you a dozen."

Finn grinned. "And I'll eat every bite." To Isaiah's back, he added, "Just don't take Clara's breath away with your manly charms."

Isaiah laughed as he hadn't been sure he'd ever be able to again. But the sound was short-lived. His steps slowed as he approached the ambulance. How was he going to find the right words to apologize to Clara for letting her down? If he'd been at the farm, she wouldn't have had to go into the stable to rescue the twins and the horse.

Sending Finn pie was an easy way to repay his debt to his friend, but how was he going to repay his debt to Clara for failing her?

Clara's heart danced in her aching chest when Isaiah heaved himself into the ambulance. The sight of his face, blackened by smoke, was the best medicine she could have. But raising her head was too much, and she began to cough.

"Whoa there," Jasmine, the other EMT, said as she put her fingers on Clara's wrist to check her pulse. "Take it easy. I can tell he makes your heart go pitter-patter, but we want your heart rate slower, not faster."

Leaning her head back on the thin pillow on the gurney, Clara nodded.

"If you promise to be good," Jasmine continued, "I'll give you time alone while I start filling out my report."

"I promise." Isaiah's hoarse voice didn't sound like his own. "And I'll make sure she's *gut*, too."

"I'm sure you will." The vehicle bounced when the EMT jumped out.

When Isaiah sat on the low stool Jasmine had been using, Clara smiled past the oxygen tubes connecting her nose and lungs to a nearby tank. He was careful not to jostle any of the IV tubes running into her left arm.

Shock made her heart skip a beat when he grabbed her left hand. She fought not to cough so she could hear what he said.

"I should have been here. I'm sorry." He pressed his forehead to her hand. "I'm so, so sorry, Clara. Please forgive me."

Her other fingers rose to brush aside the hair that fell forward onto her skin. The clatter of the IV startled her, but she ignored it. "Forgive you for what?"

"For not being here."

"But you *were* here. You saved Bella and me. We're alive because of you."

"If I'd been here, you wouldn't have had to go into the stable, and you wouldn't be lying here with these machines hooked up to you."

"Do you think you could have kept me out when the twins were inside?" She raised a single eyebrow, though the slight motion sent a pain across her head.

Her attempt at humor did not bring him a smile and fell flat because he was too caught up in his despair to hear what she said. Why? She was alive. The *kinder* were alive. The stable was gone, but not the other outbuildings or the house. Why was he insisting on punishing himself for what *hadn't* happened instead of being grateful for what had?

Then she realized what was in his head and his heart. Before she could halt herself from saying the words she didn't want to believe were true, she asked, "You think if you'd been at your house that day Rose wouldn't have died?"

"*Ja*. No. I mean—" He clamped his lips closed, but the potent emotions in his eyes burned her almost as fiercely as the fire's embers had.

"Tell me what you mean." Instinct warned her that he needed to keep talking until he broke open the half-healed scars within his heart and let out the pain infecting him.

For a long moment, he said nothing. He shifted as if he planned to get up and leave. She feared he wanted to run away again from the grief and guilt he'd carried with him for too long.

"I tried hard to keep her safe," he whispered. "I never came into the house smelling of smoke from the forge."

"I've wondered why you change clothes in the barn and wash up out there."

"Rose should never have married a blacksmith when the faintest wisp of smoke could bring on an asthma attack."

"That's easy to say, but when the heart gets involved,

gut sense goes out the window." She closed her eyes and drew in the deepest breath she could. When she began to cough, she groped for the cup of water Jasmine had left on a nearby shelf.

Isaiah pressed it into her hand. He watched as she took a drink, and she realized he would have helped her swallow past her raw throat if he could. "Are you okay?" he asked.

"I'll be if I take it easy. That's what Finn and Jasmine said."

"You should listen to them. They're skilled EMTs."

"And you should listen to me, Isaiah. How many times have you praised my common sense?"

"A lot."

"But you wouldn't have thought I had a lick of sense if you'd seen my reaction to the news my fiancé had married someone else."

A faint smile tipped the corners of his mouth. "Nobody would have faulted you for that."

"My *daed* did, but you've helped me see that he can't be other than he is. We can't change the past."

"I agree."

"Why are you trying to convince yourself Rose didn't love you when you got married?"

"Orpha said—"

"That she lied to hurt you." She pushed herself up to sit on the gurney, and the machines around her reacted to her motion. Waiting for them to calm down, she said, "It's not Orpha. It's you. *You* don't believe Rose loved you. No, you believe it, but you don't want to. You'd rather wallow in your self-loathing."

"Don't be silly. That's not what I feel."

She put her hand over his on the side of the gurney. "If

I had to guess, I'd say guilt is your protection against the heavy weight of your loss. The *kinder* have hidden their pain, and you have, too. Now they're facing it. Are you less courageous than a five-year-old or a three-year-old who is coming to accept the invitation from God to walk the path He's given them? Can't you believe as a grown man what each of those *kinder* accepts with innocent faith? God will never give us more than we can handle when we depend on Him to see us through."

When he wrapped his arms around her and leaned against her shoulder, tears running down his face, she held him close. She guessed it was the first time he'd allowed himself to cry since Rose had died over a year ago. In that time, the pain had feasted on him like a parasite. But he'd released the dam he'd built to hold in the pain, and the floodtide surging over him would help wash it away forever.

Later that evening, Clara leaned one shoulder against the frame of the door between the kitchen and the living room. She was much better, able to draw a breath without coughing. The EMTs had given her instructions to call 911 if her symptoms returned, and the paper sat in the middle of the kitchen table.

Isaiah motioned for the *kinder* to join him in the living room. His eyes were lined in red, but his shoulders seemed to have risen at least an inch as he began to set aside the burden of guilt he'd been carrying. He had many months of healing ahead of him, but, like Andrew, Ammon, Nancy and Nettie Mae, he'd begun to move in that direction.

She watched as Isaiah sat on the floor with the twins.

They eyed him uneasily, and, for once, he didn't smile to ease their concerns.

Or hers.

If the fire chief's suspicions were true, what the youngsters had done this afternoon had been far worse than forgetting to pick up their crayons or spilling a glass of milk. The twins squirmed, a sure sign of guilt. She hoped Isaiah would be gentle when he knew how virulent guilt could be. It'd nearly stolen his happiness for the rest of his life. However, she was sure of one thing: Isaiah wouldn't be like her *daed* who'd lambasted her for embarrassing him and the family with her broken betrothal. His friends had trusted him with the *kinder*, and she did, too.

"Do you want to tell me about what happened this afternoon?" he asked with the calm tone they'd learned worked best with the *kinder*.

All four exchanged uneasy glances.

Andrew spoke first. "It was an accident."

"It?" asked Isaiah.

"Fire, ain't so?" asked Nettie Mae.

"Ja." Isaiah's lips tightened, and Clara guessed he was trying not to smile at the little girl's ingenuousness. "I'm sure the fire was an accident, but who will tell me what happened?"

"I will." At Ammon's answer, Clara had to keep her smile hidden. She was grateful the little boy was taking an active part in their conversations. She wondered how much longer Andrew would be the youngsters' unchallenged leader.

"Go ahead," prompted Isaiah.

The little boy's tale was short and to the point. He and Andrew wanted to prove to their sisters that they knew how to light a lantern and decided to prove it in the stable.

"We wanted to show them we could take care of a pony, so we could get one like *Daed* promised."

She held her breath, waiting for Isaiah's response.

He asked, "And?"

"We took the matches out of the drawer when Clara wasn't looking." Ammon blinked back tears as he turned to her. "We're sorry, Clara, for touching things we shouldn't have."

"I know." She didn't want to interrupt the conversation.

"We tried to stomp the fire out," Nancy said.

Clara bit her lip to keep her gasp of dismay from erupting. If one of the *kinder*'s clothing had caught fire, the fire would have become a true tragedy. She murmured a soft prayer of gratitude to God for watching over the twins and saving them from their folly.

"Pieces of hay and fire went everywhere," Andrew added. "That's when we got scared."

"So you ran, Andrew?" Isaiah asked.

The boy nodded.

"And you hid?" Isaiah focused on the girls.

They nodded.

"And I went to get Bella," Ammon said, "but couldn't find her in the smoke."

"We're thankful we found you *and* Bella in the smoke." He leaned toward them. "What you did was very dangerous. Any of you—and Clara—could have died. You must never touch matches without permission again until you're big enough."

"No more," Nancy said.

Her twin nodded and reached for her braid to chew on. Clara had meant to help her break that habit, but she was glad Nettie Mae had its comfort. Next week, if she was still there next week, she'd start working with the little girl to convince her to stop putting her hair in her mouth.

"And we keep our promises," Andrew said, sticking out his chest in a pose he must have thought made him look grown up.

"Gut," Isaiah said. "This is one you *must* keep."

"We will." Ammon rose to his knees. "We'll keep it like we've kept our promise to *Mamm* when she said no more laughing."

Clara heard a choked sound from Isaiah and knew he was as astounded as she was. Not once had she imagined the twins' *mamm* had been the one to order them not to laugh. She squatted so her eyes were level with the *kinder*'s. "When did she say that?"

"Before she and *Daed* left and didn't come home," Ammon said. Thick tears welled up in his eyes.

As Clara held him close, trying to offer him what solace she could, she wondered if the misunderstanding had arisen because Esta was worried about being late and had tried to keep the youngsters quiet so she could finish whatever she needed to do before she and Melvin left for the auction. How many words had she herself said in haste and come to rue afterward? But, at least, what had been done could be undone.

She looked over Ammon's head to where Isaiah was comforting the other three. "Your *mamm* and *daed* want you to laugh whenever you want to for the rest of your lives. The sound of laughter is very light, and it reaches all the way up to them in heaven."

"They hear us laughing?" asked Nettie Mae.

"Ja, so laugh when you want to, because your parents will be happy to hear you."

"I gonna." The little girl raised her chin. "Lots and lots."

Isaiah's gaze caught hers, and she saw his sorrow matched her own. But she also saw in his eyes hope for better times ahead and knew they were on their way to healing their hearts.

"Whew!" Isaiah said as he came down the stairs along with Clara after putting the *kinder* to bed. "I wasn't sure if we'd get them to sleep."

"It's been a tough day for them."

"For everyone." He gave her a half smile as he curled an arm around her shoulders as they went toward the kitchen. "One of the worst days of my life, but also one of the best because this house will ring with childish laughter soon." He opened the door to the *dawdi haus*. As he started to bid her to have a *gut* night's rest, he paused and said, "Oh, I forgot about this."

She watched while he went to the table and picked up an envelope. Handing it to her, he said nothing. Her eyes widened when she saw the international stamps on it.

"From the *kinder*'s grandparents?" she asked.

"*Ja.* We can read it tonight and share it with them in the morning, if you'd like."

"That's a *gut* idea." She opened it, pulled out the pages inside and began to read aloud:

"'Dear Andrew, Ammon, Nancy, Nettie Mae, Isaiah and Clara,

'First, we want to thank you for the *wunderbaar* pictures and stories about the *kinder*. We've received each letter with joy. It's such a blessing to get to know our *kins-kinder* better. We wish we had more time with you.

'And that brings us to something we want to address to you, Isaiah. As you may or may not know, we haven't had the amount of time we would have liked to spend with our *kins-kinder*. Our call to serve has taken us to many places, and our visits to our son and his family have been few and far between. Melvin was concerned about his *kinder* not knowing us. He mentioned that when he spoke with us before he asked you, Isaiah, to serve as guardian for the twins if anything happened to him. We know he asked you to assist Esta in his place. Hearing you agreed to both without hesitation has told us much about the man you are. A *gut* man and a God-fearing one who has served his Lord to the best of his abilities, and a man who wouldn't shirk his duties to his friend's family.

'Clara, we have come to know you through your kind letters, which have filled our hearts with joy. The twins' lives have been made better by you being in them, we're sure. But we know you're there only temporarily.

'A long-term solution must be found for the *kinder*. We cannot bring them here to live with us, and from what we've heard from Debra Wittmer, she's in a similar situation. Our love for our *kins-kinder* will never change, but, Isaiah, would you consider taking them permanently? They need a *gut* home and a *gut daed*. We believe you can provide that home and be their *daed*.'"

Clara lowered the letter and whispered, "Did I read that right? They want you to adopt the twins?"

"That's what it sounded like to me." He started to grin. "I'm glad it sounded that way to you, too."

"Do you think it's possible?" she asked, wondering what the *kinder* would say when they heard of this. She prayed they wouldn't feel unwanted by their grandparents and *aenti* as she'd felt unwanted by her *daed* for too many years.

"*Ja*, it's possible for the Amish to adopt. My sister, Esther, and her husband have."

She shook her head. "I wasn't talking about the legalities. I meant is this something *you* want to do? Do you want to change from a temporary *daed* to a permanent one? It's such a responsibility, Isaiah."

"I can do it, but I'll need help."

"Your family—"

"Your help, Clara." He grasped her hands, lacing his fingers through hers. "Nothing has changed."

"I can stay as long as you need me."

"But you didn't let me ask first."

"Ask what? You said you needed my help, and I'm glad to give it."

He shook his head. "Stop being scared of disappointing me as your *daed* has made you believe you've disappointed him, Clara. Listen to your heart. If you won't, then listen to mine."

Her breath caught as she realized what he was saying. She'd been caught up in wondering how the *kinder* would react to the news and hadn't thought of anything else. Certainly nothing as *wunderbaar* as what she believed he was asking of her.

His smile widened. "Clara, are you willing to go from temporary nanny to permanent *mamm* and wife? My wife?"

"Are you sure?"

"More sure than I've been of anything in my life. I

have been praying for the right time to propose, and I think this is it. I'm not asking because of the *kinder*. I'm asking because I love you. Do you love me?"

"With all my heart…except for the part that belongs to four mischievous twins."

"I can offer you almost all my heart…everything except for what belongs to four imps. But you haven't given me your answer, Clara. Will you marry me?"

"*Ja*, I'll marry you."

He let out a whoop, then glanced toward the ceiling. "I hope I didn't wake them before I can…" He caressed her cheek, and she slanted her face into his warm palm.

When his mouth found hers, she knew she'd never understood the breadth of happiness until this moment. They still had a lot of grief to deal with, but they'd be doing it together.

Laughter sounded around them, and Isaiah pulled away. In shock, she saw the twins giggling with the ease she'd prayed for.

"What's funny?" Isaiah asked in a feigned gruff voice.

"Kissing is funny," shouted Andrew before dissolving into laughter again. The other twins joined in.

"You've got it almost right." Isaiah drew her into his arms once more. "Kissing isn't funny. It's fun." And to prove his point, he kissed her again and again until they were laughing as hard as the youngsters.

Epilogue

Clara brought another tray with two pitchers of freshly squeezed lemonade. She set them on the tables in the middle of the yard before admiring how much of the new stable had been already rebuilt. There were fewer volunteers than for a full barn raising, but the new stable would be finished before dark tonight except for a coat of paint to match the barn. The smoke stains there were covered by the new white paint.

Esther and Ruth walked over to the table. They were the only two of Isaiah's siblings she hadn't met before, because they lived too far away for easy visits when Ruth had a young baby and Esther was very pregnant.

"Perfect timing," Esther said. "The men were talking about taking a break and hoped you were making something *gut* to drink."

"Tell them to *komm* and get it!" she replied with a laugh.

Esther cupped her hands over her mouth and shouted, "Lemonade!" At Clara's shock, she laughed. "I used to be a schoolteacher. I know how to be heard."

Cheers met the announcement, and the men put aside their tools before hurrying to the table to quench the thirsts they'd been working up on the hot, humid day.

Clara smiled when Isaiah moved close to her and smiled. "I heard some interesting news."

"Not more rumors, I hope."

He gave an emoted shudder, then chuckled. "I got this news right from the horse's mouth."

"That's no way to talk about your *mamm*." Wanda wagged a finger at him, and everyone laughed.

"What's the news, Isaiah?" asked Esther. "You can't leave us hanging like clothes on a line."

"Do you want to tell them, *Mamm*, Reuben?" asked Isaiah.

Reuben grinned and said, "Wanda and I will be publishing our intentions to marry in October."

More cheers erupted, and everyone was hugging everyone else.

Isaiah took Clara's hand and drew her away from the crowd. Out of earshot, he said, "I hope you're not disappointed that we won't be the next one to get married."

"As long as we get married."

"Let's get married two weeks after Reuben and *Mamm*. It'll give everyone time to prepare for a second wedding, and we should be able to get in a few visits to family before the adoption proceedings begin."

"Those can't be started until the relinquishment of parental rights paperwork is signed by Melvin's parents and Debra."

"It'll be soon, and then you'll be a wife and a *mamm*."

She put her arms around his neck, not caring if anyone saw them. "And you'll be my forever husband and their forever *daed*."

"There's nothing I want to be more." He confirmed that with a kiss.

* * * * *

Don't miss these other AMISH HEARTS *stories
from Jo Ann Brown:*

*AMISH HOMECOMING
AN AMISH MATCH
HIS AMISH SWEETHEART
AN AMISH REUNION*

Find more great reads at www.LoveInspired.com

Dear Reader,

The fear of letting go can keep us from enjoying the moment we're living right now. Both Clara and Isaiah take on the task of caring for four orphaned children, knowing that soon they will need to hand those children over to members of their extended family. Learning to live every minute and trusting that God is leading them in the direction they must go is a lesson they—and all of us—must learn. I would like to think I would be as willing to love deeply and then let go as Clara and Isaiah are, but anyone who has lost someone dear to them knows that can be the most difficult part of life.

Stop in and visit me at *www.joannbrownbooks.com* Look for my next story in the *Amish Hearts* series coming soon.

Wishing you many blessings,
Jo Ann Brown

COMING NEXT MONTH FROM
Love Inspired®

Available May 23, 2017

THEIR PRETEND AMISH COURTSHIP
The Amish Bachelors • by Patricia Davids

To avoid their matchmaking mothers' plans and pursue their dreams, Fannie Erb and Noah Bowman agree to a pretend courtship. As they make room in their schedules to attend events as a couple, could their hearts also begin to make room for each other?

LONE STAR BACHELOR
The Buchanons • by Linda Goodnight

Content with his bachelor life, builder Sawyer Buchanon's world is turned upside down when he meets pretty PI Jade Warren. Jade was raised to never trust a Buchanon, but when she's hired to investigate the vandalism at Sawyer's building projects, the Texas charmer soon sweeps her off her feet.

SECOND-CHANCE COWBOY
Cowboys of Cedar Ridge • by Carolyne Aarsen

Once she's paid off her father's debts, Tabitha Rennie plans to leave Cedar Ridge and all the painful memories it brings. Having ex-fiancé Morgan Walsh ask for help connecting with his son was not part of the plan. Yet spending time with father and son is creating dreams of house and home.

FALLING FOR THE RANCHER
Aspen Creek Crossroads • by Roxanne Rustand

As a single mom, veterinarian Darcy Leighton would do anything for her daughter—including remaining at the clinic with rancher vet Logan Maxwell, the man who bought the place out from under her. As they work together, their truce turns to friendship—and to the discovery of a once-in-a-lifetime love.

THE SINGLE MOM'S SECOND CHANCE
Goose Harbor • by Jessica Keller

Returning to Goose Harbor, Claire Atwood has plenty of reasons for staying away from Evan Daniels—most notably being jilted at the altar by her onetime sweetheart. But both are running for mayor, which means spending time together. But could it also mean a second chance at forever?

HOMETOWN HERO'S REDEMPTION
by Jill Kemerer

When rugged firefighter Drew Gannon asks her to babysit troubled ten-year-old Wyatt, Lauren Pierce can't help but recall their high school rivalry. Can the temporary single dad prove to the pretty former social worker he's no longer the foolhardy teen she once knew—and he's actually her perfect match?

LOOK FOR THESE AND OTHER LOVE INSPIRED BOOKS WHEREVER BOOKS ARE SOLD, INCLUDING MOST BOOKSTORES, SUPERMARKETS, DISCOUNT STORES AND DRUGSTORES.

LICNM0517

Get 2 Free Books,

Plus 2 Free Gifts—

just for trying the Reader Service!

YES! Please send me 2 FREE Love Inspired® Romance novels and my 2 FREE mystery gifts (gifts are worth about $10 retail). After receiving them, if I don't wish to receive any more books, I can return the shipping statement marked "cancel." If I don't cancel, I will receive 6 brand-new novels every month and be billed just $5.24 for the regular-print edition or $5.74 each for the larger-print edition in the U.S., or $5.74 each for the regular-print edition or $6.24 each for the larger-print edition in Canada. That's a saving of at least 13% off the cover price. It's quite a bargain! Shipping and handling is just 50¢ per book in the U.S. and 75¢ per book in Canada.* I understand that accepting the 2 free books and gifts places me under no obligation to buy anything. I can always return a shipment and cancel at any time. Even if I never buy another book, the 2 free books and gifts are mine to keep forever.

Please check one:

☐ Love Inspired Romance Regular-Print
   (105/305 IDN GLQC)

☐ Love Inspired Romance Larger-Print
   (122/322 IDN GLQD)

Name	(PLEASE PRINT)	
Address		Apt. #
City	State/Province	Zip/Postal Code

Signature (if under 18, a parent or guardian must sign)

Mail to the **Reader Service:**
IN U.S.A.: P.O. Box 1867, Buffalo, NY 14240-1867
IN CANADA: P.O. Box 611, Fort Erie, Ontario L2A 9Z9

Want to try two free books from another line?
Call 1-800-873-8635 today or visit www.ReaderService.com.

*Terms and prices subject to change without notice. Prices do not include applicable taxes. Sales tax applicable in N.Y. Canadian residents will be charged applicable taxes. Offer not valid in Quebec. This offer is limited to one order per household. Books received may not be as shown. Not valid for current subscribers to Love Inspired Romance books. All orders subject to credit approval. Credit or debit balances in a customer's account(s) may be offset by any other outstanding balance owed by or to the customer. Please allow 4 to 6 weeks for delivery. Offer available while quantities last.

Your Privacy—The Reader Service is committed to protecting your privacy. Our Privacy Policy is available online at www.ReaderService.com or upon request from the Reader Service.

We make a portion of our mailing list available to reputable third parties that offer products we believe may interest you. If you prefer that we not exchange your name with third parties, or if you wish to clarify or modify your communication preferences, please visit us at www.ReaderService.com/consumerchoice or write to us at Reader Service Preference Service, P.O. Box 9062, Buffalo, NY 14240-9062. Include your complete name and address.

LI17R

SPECIAL EXCERPT FROM

Love Inspired®

*Will a pretend courtship fend off matchmaking mothers,
or will it lead to true love?*

Read on for a sneak preview of
THEIR PRETEND AMISH COURTSHIP,
the next book in **Patricia Davids**'s
heartwarming series, **AMISH BACHELORS**.

"Noah, where are you? I need to speak to you."

Working near the back of his father's barn, Noah Bowman dropped the hoof of his buggy horse Willy, took the last nail out of his mouth and stood upright to stare over his horse's back. Fannie Erb, his neighbor's youngest daughter, came hurrying down the wide center aisle, checking each stall as she passed. Her white *kapp* hung off the back of her head dangling by a single bobby pin. Her curly red hair was still in a bun, but it was windblown and lopsided. No doubt, it would be completely undone before she got home. Fannie was always in a rush.

"What's up, *karotte oben*?" He picked up his horse's hoof again, positioned it between his knees and drove in the last nail of the new shoe.

Fannie stopped outside the stall gate and fisted her hands on her hips. "You know I hate being called a carrot top."

"Sorry." Noah grinned.

LIEXP0517

He wasn't sorry a bit. He liked the way her unusual violet eyes darkened and flashed when she was annoyed. Annoying Fannie had been one of his favorite pastimes when they were schoolchildren.

Framed as she was in a rectangle of light cast by the early-morning sun shining through the open top of a Dutch door, dust motes danced around Fannie's head like fireflies drawn to the fire in her hair. The summer sun had expanded the freckles on her upturned nose and given her skin a healthy glow, but Fannie didn't tan the way most women did. Her skin always looked cool and creamy. As usual, she was wearing blue jeans and riding boots under her plain green dress and black apron.

"What you need, Fannie? Did your hot temper spark a fire and you want me to put it out?" He chuckled at his own wit. He along with his four brothers were volunteer members of the local fire department.

"This isn't a joke, Noah. I need to get engaged, and quickly. Will you help me?"

Don't miss
THEIR PRETEND AMISH COURTSHIP
by Patricia Davids, available June 2017 wherever
Love Inspired® books and ebooks are sold.

www.LoveInspired.com

Copyright © 2017 by Patricia MacDonald

LIEXP0517

EXCLUSIVE LIMITED TIME OFFER AT
www.HARLEQUIN.com

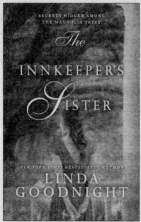

$15.99 U.S./$18.99 CAN.

$1.⁵⁰ OFF

New York Times Bestselling Author

LINDA GOODNIGHT

welcomes you to Honey Ridge, Tennessee, where long-buried secrets lead to some startling realizations in

Available April 25, 2017
Get your copy today!

Receive $1.50 OFF the purchase price of THE INNKEEPER'S SISTER by Linda Goodnight when you use the coupon code below on Harlequin.com

SISTERS17

Offer valid from April 25, 2017, until May 31, 2017, on www.Harlequin.com.

Valid in the U.S.A. and Canada only. To redeem this offer, please add the print or ebook version of THE INNKEEPER'S SISTER by Linda Goodnight to your shopping cart and then enter the coupon code at checkout.

DISCLAIMER: Offer valid on the print or ebook version of THE INNKEEPER'S SISTER by Linda Goodnight from April 25, 2017, at 12:01 a.m. ET until May 31, 2017, 11:59 p.m. ET at www.Harlequin.com only. The Customer will receive $1.50 OFF the list price of THE INNKEEPER'S SISTER by Linda Goodnight in print or ebook on www.Harlequin.com with the SISTERS17 coupon code. Sales tax applied where applicable. Quantities are limited. Valid in the U.S.A. and Canada only. All orders subject to approval.

www.HQNBooks.com

® and ™ are trademarks owned and used by the trademark owner and/or its licensee.
© 2017 Harlequin Enterprises Limited

PHCOUPLGLI0517

Turn your love of reading into rewards you'll love with
Harlequin My Rewards

**Join for FREE today at
www.HarlequinMyRewards.com**

Earn **FREE BOOKS** of your choice.

Experience **EXCLUSIVE OFFERS** and contests.

Enjoy **BOOK RECOMMENDATIONS**
selected just for you.

PLUS! Sign up now
and get **500** points
right away!

Earn
FREE
REWARDS
Join
Today!
HarlequinMyRewards.com

MYR16R